Gas Station

Joseph Torra is the author of *Keep Watching the Sky*, a collection of poetry. He lives in Somerville, Massachusetts.

By the same author
Keep Watching the Sky (poetry)

Gas Station

JOSEPH TORRA

VICTOR GOLLANCZ

LONDON

First published in the USA in 1996 by Zoland Books, Inc.

A Gollancz Paperback Original
First published in Great Britain in 1999
by Victor Gollancz
An imprint of Orion Books Ltd,
Orion House, 5 Upper St Martin's Lane,
London WC2H 9EA

A CIP catalogue record for this book is
available from the British Library.

ISBN 0 575 06803 5

Printed and bound in Great Britain by
The Guernsey Press Co. Ltd, Guernsey, C.I.

For Lucille and Betty

Gas Station

I'M BURNING TRASH piece by piece tossing take-out coffee cups, crumpled sandwich paper, paper bags, pizza boxes, donut boxes, this morning's *Record American* into the rusty fifty-gallon drum holes punched through sides for ventilation. Cigarette butts I glean and smoke stirring the black-smoke paper fire. It smells back here where Countess is chained up all day her shits sit various stages of decay. Stacks of burned-out engines, transmissions and rear-ends exude sludgy streams of stale motor oil, transmission and rear-end fluids. Nothing smells foul as rear-end fluid. The labyrinth drains into a wide puddle inches thick black muck hottest days reeks like death. Keep an eye out says he'll break my legs catches me smoking he'll smack me around a bit, yell a hell of a lot, but won't come back here too lazy he'll holler haven't heard the hose bell ring no one at the pumps. What's the best gas I ask something stupid what do you mean what's the best gas Jenney's the best gas I know Jenney's the best gas what's the best Jenney gas, regular or premium? Premium he shouts premium's the best gas that's why it costs more. Regular's 28 and $^9/_{10}$th cents per gallon premium 32 $^9/_{10}$th cents four cents a gallon better. Blue 1965 Chevy Impala just out of the showroom new lines for the Impala not so square as the '64 more streamlined, sleek, this one with one of those new vinyl tops at first look like convertible tops but it's hard what's the point for looks. Sporty car for old Mr. Woods just retired paid cash orders his usual five gallons I start to pump the old man washes the windshield looks the car over says too much of a loss soon as you buy a new car his one concrete reason to dismiss something now cars beginning to come equipped with seat belts he won't use 'em because he read of an accident a car caught fire the driver unable to unfasten the seat belt burned to death now he uses that as an excuse to dismiss seat belts. Never actually looked *under* a brand-new car put the gas nozzle automatic low down on my hands and knees spotless shiny configuration of undercarriage. The gas tank is cool to touch, the spotless tailpipe burns my fingertips, up front a gleaming oil pan and red-orange engine block, black transmission hospital clean eventually to be rust grease and grime myriad of leaky valves, seals, gaskets, hoses, fuel lines brake lines water lines slowly manifest with time. He's yelling I forgot the gas already gone over ten gallons what the hell are you doing I wanted to see what it looks like under there what do you think it looks like under there. Mr. Woods insists paying the difference my father won't hear of it turns on me soon as Mr. Woods leaves yelling how much I just cost him got to learn to pay attention this is a business.

FREDDY GOLAR AND "Red" Duncan blasting a pint between them long two- and three-bubble sips wash down with cold Pepsi thick twisty rolled glass bottles I stock in the machine. They cough and ooch it doesn't take them ten minutes finish and commence to hoe-down Red slapping air bass on broomstick Freddy air violin fiddling. Red's "Red" because Red's wavy shiny red hair orange-freckle-ridden complexion when he drinks his face burns bright red his eyes flame. Red's big and solid with muscular tattooed arms fit from years working in the tunnels down from Prince Edward Island with his brothers James and Joe digging the Callahan Tunnel James dies in a tunnel fire someone lights a cigarette where they shouldn't. Joe tells stories of his days digging the tunnels Red never does Red's singing laughing Freddy puts his fiddle down combs his thick white hair over his face nearly reaches his mouth dancing in circles clapping his hands. Don't know how old Freddy is married forty years no children now he's drunk tells me again about overseas in the service he fought with a crazy Italian soldier who grabbed hard hold of his balls twisted his scrotum around his leg and made him sterile. His wife calls calls again third call he goes. Red's only getting started won't see him after tonight for a week or longer out on a tear lives in the house behind the station with Joe and their mother. There's always someone hanging around the station picking up a little work as a gofer or cleaning cars on the

side or having a good time like Freddy and Red.
I bum cigarettes off them company helps pass the
time my father trusts me alone with the station
at night he's at the dog track playing cards maybe
with a woman.

FEW MECHANICS MASTERS Lenny Barns no master.
Lanky Lenny mug shot eyes greased hair combed
back pointed pockmarked face chain-smoking
Camels grabs me by my ears says like two loving
cup handles pulls my head down between his legs
wrap your lips around it it'll only take me a few
seconds never sure whether he really means it he's
got the most beautiful red-haired wife. Tortures
Countess when the old man's not around ties
things around her head laughs at her struggling
to free herself grabs the shotgun from the compressor room loads it chases me into the garage
hide behind a stack of tires sudden BLAST concrete fragments fall on my head. Says he was a
mechanic for Connie Kalitta national drag racing champ the Zona brothers tell me Lenny never
knew Connie Kalitta. Lenny quits shortly after

the fire I'm home and Michael Mackey from down the street with ten brothers and sisters screaming the gas station blew up and he's got half his brothers and sisters with him and they're hollering the gas station blew up. Lenny's smoking while pumping gas blown back in the initial blast knocked off his feet shouts to Doctor Bagsarian who's still sitting in the burning car get out and the doctor gets out and away in the nick of time. For days everybody talks about the fire the station closes for several days the *Mercury* runs articles front-page photo Lenny sitting at our kitchen table Lenny tells the story how it blew tossed him the fuck back like a bug same story he tells the newspaperman or me or customers or anyone who will listen fervor like he really enjoys what happened and telling the story over and over changes slightly more polish and drama each telling. The *Mercury* photo sitting dazed at our kitchen table face and hands bandaged, eyes awry, double shots of whiskey Lenny.

GAS STATION

OAK STREET'S A connector street allows Malden
and Melrose traffic access to Interstate 93 and
Route 28. Before this is a gas station it's a vari-
ety store old-timers remember cigarettes eight
cents a pack. In 1949 huge holes are dug for gasoline storage tanks, new piping and a pump island
installed, an outside pit's dug down where a mechanic climbs automobiles driven over him. The
two-car garage out back's soon built woodstove
heat during winter and wet weather now only
used for storage then a one-car garage is attached
to the office a lift installed pit outside filled in.
Still later another one-car garage added onto the
first space limitations won't allow the garages next
to each other but one in front of the other long
garage two years ago my father with the help of
Bill Gleason gets a second lift installed in newer
back half of the garage so when it's busy we can
keep several jobs going at once. There are houses
on each side of the property in which the Wiggins,
De Franco, Hart and Maynard families live
though the Maynard family's only old Clyde
who's eighty-seven and his younger brother Ralph
who's eighty both retired railroad workers still
wearing their engineer's caps. Traffic's light on

Oak Street except during morning and afternoon rush not busy enough to sustain good gas business most gas customers regulars from neighborhood. My father's ignored by the Jenney Company because of the company's obligation to the higher-volume stations at the same time they're not around as often with their noses in his business as they are at big-volume places which my father says is fine. Look closely discern uneven patchwork various building sections first garage red brick is melded with stucco office structure second garage concrete blocks makeshift fit to red brick first garage outside the building painted white with red trim big blue J E N N E Y letters above office picture window. Over the years learn cars and faces people who drive by tired bleary-eyed morning traffic stream late afternoon early evening yawn return. Imagine spacious houses, quiet green lawn shrubbery streets in Melrose, children who own their own skis eat dinners of beef gravy potatoes desserts day's events discussed over oversized glasses of milk. Families of Saturday morning drive by, skis attached to roof racks winter, summer's beach chairs and coolers towing boats and campers to Newfound Lake New

Hampshire or Bar Harbor Maine. Country Squire wood-grain station wagons, new blue four-doors.

BLIZZARD OF '68 midnight plow all evening drive home old '48 Willy's Jeep plow piston breaks plow stuck down turn around head back to the station if we can make it fix it in the morning. Snow swarms through headlights' view, rolls over top of the plow in waves little truck grinds forward a tank the old man says. Turn off the Fellsway up Oak can we make the hill lucky not to burn out motor or transmission four wheels spinning broken tire chains slapping into the station lot sleep in the garage, rubber-tire beds, fender guards for blankets. Morning snow drifts five six feet high across the station lot still snowing radio stations on storm emergency Blackie fixes the plow piston I shovel two-feet-wide strip around pump island, another two feet away from the building, my father plows one long pile into bigger piles ten feet high front and rear of the station. Interstate 93 closed blocked hundreds of cars abandoned must be cleared for plow trucks most of the abandoned cars are locked we have to struggle with a coat hanger to get the doors open Blackie and I returning to the station in the tow truck with a car on the boom my father's broken English over the radio WBZ emergency hotline tella de people no locka de cars whenday leavem onnada highway we laugh out loud tella de people no locka de cars Blackie mocks. We tow twenty-four hours straight thirty-three cars in the lot nowhere to put more my father charges twenty-five for the tow fifteen a day storage some argue too much but want their cars back and pay.

PINUPS IN THE compressor room a blond sitting in a wicker chair holding an ice-cream cone, pig-tailed brunette woman in cheerleader skirt and socks looks like Sally Field think she is Sally Field I watch *Gidget* can't tell. Calendar out back by the tire machine courtesy Riverside Auto Parts redheaded woman with large breasts who burned two black spots where her nipples should be hangs here the whole year. George arrives with coffee and donuts shows us a magazine pictures of a woman having sex with a pig look at that curly little tail Joe says laughing Tommy and George tell me look closely that's how it's done son, that's how it's done. Pig looks a bit like Annie they laugh George says hasn't stopped you Joe Tommy you neither. One night working alone Annie comes in for gas in the front seat Billy Coniglio from my seventh-grade class next day at school ask him he goes out with her isn't she old so what. George says Annie ain't pretty but ain't she pretty fat.

SIX-FIFTEEN A.M. he wakes me wash and dress stop on the way Town Line Donuts buzzing with city workers, cops, Freddy from Freddy's Sunoco. All the guys crazy for Willa and Cookie's two daughters Willa and Cookie own the Town Line their two daughters a few years older I never keep my mind on what I'm ordering. Sometimes I get two honey-dipped with coffee today a bacon and egg sandwich takes a little longer she has to make it over the grill short hemline on the uniform she leans over the grill to flip the egg she's got legs all the way up to her ass Freddy says to me I nod

my head yes but doesn't everyone? We open at
seven before I eat turn on the pumps and compressor, bring out the tires in the little B. F.
Goodrich tire stands, jacks, windshield wiper
center, roll out the hose for the bell. Two bites
into my sandwich someone pulls in for gas or
leaves a car for work morning's busiest time my
father's already barking out orders for me Blackie
figures out what parts we need for various jobs
the old man off for several hours chasing them
while I work the pumps Blackie takes it all apart.
In between gas customers hang out and talk with
Blackie lets me smoke his cigarettes he's got a
1955 Chevy Bel Air red and white cherry clean
showroom stock a biker rode with the Disciples
his wife looks like a pinup girl made him quit
biking though once after he quit and sold his bike
she saw him riding down the Revere Beach Parkway at the head of a pack with a girl on his back.
Blackie has a brother Billy and the Zona brothers kind of famous locally since Billy owned a fuel
dragster raced for two seasons at New England
Dragway placed third in finals once now it's in
need of much work sits rusting in the garage at
Billy's parents' house. The fastest I ever went in

a car was in Billy's '54 Ford Skyline with pearl
green paint job full-blown 312 V-8 Billy rebuilt
from a wrecked '56 Ford Interstate 93 130 miles
an hour pinned to my black leather bucket seat
Billy ripping madly through those gears. The old
man's back 10:30 after coffee I help Blackie with
an exhaust system a '58 Pontiac Chieftain later I
sit in a '59 Caddy with the huge tail fins up on
the lift await Blackie's instructions to pump the
brake pedal so he can bleed the brake cylinders.
Long minutes up here stare out at rows of tires
in storage to my right and long row fan belts and
radiator hoses hanging to my left. I turn on the
car radio 'RKO or 'BZ Beatles maybe Gerry and
the Pacemakers Roy Orbison "Pretty Woman."
I think about Willa and Cookie's daughters my
dick hardens Blackie shouts shut the fucking radio I can't hear him when he tells me to pump.
By noon most of the work finished my father goes
out for subs I take a meatball Blackie's a fussy
eater roast beef cooked on the grill with may-
onnaise when we get pizza he takes his cheese and
pepperoni off eats with sauce only I put his cheese
and pepperoni on top of my slices. Old man naps
after lunch pulls the tow truck around back sleeps

in there Blackie finishes up the last of his work then pulls his '55 Chevy into the garage lets me grease it and change the oil. We turn the radio up and smoke Blackie listens to 1950s music his friend Phil who drives a '63 green Corvette Stingray says that was music you could really make a broad to. Temperature's climbing kids I know from school walk up to the pond for swim Blackie and Phil check out the girls whistle and catcall. Wow Phil says Phil always says wow Angela Gambini passes by in her red bikini — wow — slowly and emphatically — W - A - O - U - W. Three o'clock work's finished old man's out getting iced coffees all the kids parading down the hill from the pond to catch the bus. Tonight we eat here my mother brings supper around 4:30 after Blackie leaves, a loaf of Vienna bread two pots separately wrapped in kitchen towels one for each of us sausage vinegar peppers fried potatoes still steaming from the kitchen ten minutes away the old man drinks ice water I drink Pepsi ice cold. He leaves around 6:00 got some errands to run says he'll be back in time to close at 9:00 and he always is.

MY FATHER'S NERVOUS new Registry officer's here to make sure the station's ready for the upcoming inspection season and if so drop off the little boxes of gold — inspection stickers. Johnny the MDC cop who hangs around the station drinking coffee talking about pussy with the guys says the new Registry cop's a real prick Registry cops got the easiest job in the world no need for them to be such assholes. Larry the old Registry officer's been transferred this new guy sweats fat his black hair's parted on the side greased thick into a wave he's short and round in blue and gray Registry uniform he inflates more than wears. The old man offers him two bottles of expensive Scotch Larry used to like but he refuses doesn't drink says if the old man wants to do him something he can always throw him a little something so he might take the wife out for a dinner the old man on the defensive fumbles to remove cash from his pocket officer tells him it can wait until the next time. The officer checks that the big white headlight board is clean unobstructed and in its place at the end of the garage and it is I painted it myself along with the thick yellow strip on the floor to help drivers guide themselves in. He quizzes

Blackie tries to trick him up with his questions contradicts some things Blackie says watches Blackie jack up the front end of a car check for wheel play possible loose ball joint or faulty tie-rod end. They talk allowances of eighths-of-inches play, headlights, brake lights, directional lights, horns, wipers, brakes, tire-tread depths and the officer seems pleased enough leaves the stickers says he might check back during inspection time to see how things are going. The old man after he leaves can you believe that son of a bitch a little something so he can take his wife for dinner?

PHONE CALL FROM the State Police car out of gas on Interstate 93 when we arrive the trooper takes my father aside tells him the guy out of gas has no money his license plate's from Tennessee they're running a check on him. In the meantime the old man tells me to gas him up I grab the five-gallon can out of the back of the tow truck empty its contents into the gas tank of the man's old Plymouth station wagon. The police find no reason to detain him a matter of how the guy can

pay for the gas he looks dazed his eyes glazed like
he hasn't slept in days he's got a watch takes it
off shows it to the old man the old man says
follow us back to the station just off the next exit
we'll fill your car up and figure something out.
At the station I fill him up ask where he's from
Tennessee my father asks how he ended up strand-
ed with no money he was supposed to get work
in Maine and it fell through he was on his way
back to Tennessee. Blackie and I are amused listening to my father and this man from Tennessee
converse my father's Italian broken English and
this guy's rebel accent so thick talks so low every
time he says anything have to ask him to repeat
what he said and he and my father misunderstand-
ing what the other one says by the time their
verbal exchange is finished the conclusion each
has arrived at is completely erroneous. One thing
we all understand is that the man hasn't eaten
since yesterday when he had three donuts my
father takes twenty bucks out of the cash regis-
ter gives it to him leave the watch when you get
to where you're going mail the money we'll mail
back the watch. My father thinks the watch is
worth some money when the man leaves he puts

it in the locked drawer where he keeps the inspection stickers remains there years each time I see it I see the Tennessean's beaten face, bad teeth, tattered clothes and glassy eyes.

ALWAYS SOME KIND of payoff he's doing a favor for someone or someone's doing a favor for him. Always a license or permit or stretch of road you can bargain for my father's the stretch of Interstate 93 from the Medford/Somerville line north to the intersection with 128. His friend Tom Riordan secured him that stretch of towing rights my father does more favors for Tom than anybody else. Tom was a member of the state House of Representatives now has an official job on the state payroll perpetually deals a hand my father's ever eager to grab so my father has rights to all the road service and towing work on three and a half to four miles of Interstate 93 through the favor system and bringing expensive whiskey and beer to the State Police barracks once every month. He drags me along with him so I can carry the cases of booze up the barracks stairs he acts

like an ass with the troopers thinks he's just one
of the guys retells the same story the time he was
servicing a car up on 93 and a speeding passing
car tore the open door off of Trooper Lopez's
cruiser and the car never stopped. We leave the
booze and for the next several weeks the towing
business booms then slowly trails off until someone spies the tow truck from Sonny's Mobil
towing our stretch of road then the old man goes
out buys more cases expensive booze and beer and
we make our pilgrimage to the barracks again.

GO DOWN THE Jew's and get me some cream he
says handing me a dollar bill every day drinks
cream for his bad stomach every day cream and
Maalox cream and Maalox. He won't go into
Harry's store claims one time Harry overcharged
him for something every time I go into Harry's
Harry tells me *his* version of the story. Most
people in the neighborhood call Harry Harry the
Jew and his store Harry the Jew's I call him Harry
and the store Harry's he's a friendly man wise in
ways knows locals don't like him call him Harry

the Jew he has an IF I CAN'T TAKE IT WITH ME I'M
NOT GOING sign up brown and curling around the
edges feeds right in with my father's belief that
Jews are money misers but that sign means more
about living than money says Harry. Harry used
to sell and repair bicycles now with all the de-
partment stores around it's been years since
anyone bought a new bike from Harry and he's
still got a couple of dusty fat-tired bulky boys'
bikes you don't see much anymore with all the
new streamlined stingrays and ten-speeds. Harry
still fixes a few bikes, sells some milk, cigarettes
or candy but if the store wasn't the downstairs
part of his house I don't think he could afford to
stay open though he's not really open usually he's
upstairs when I enter a little bell rings up there
in a minute or two Harry's footsteps descend the
creaky wooden stairs, never in any hurry Harry
with the cigar stub in his mouth wearing baggy
brown pants, white wrinkled shirt and ill-fitting
tie, old gray button-down wool sweater, balding
scruffy gray head of hair, thick eyeglasses I try
to look him in the eye but the round brown balls
blur says my father never liked him no one else
in the neighborhood either he can't understand

treats everyone fairly always has I tell Harry
people are funny that way Harry says it's closed
minds. Usually I get a Ring Ding or Devil Dogs
with the change eat them on the walk back to the
station the old man glugs down half the carton
of cream puts the rest in the Pepsi machine which
doubles as a refrigerator sits back down at his
desk belches for a few minutes holding his stomach and groaning in pain, looking at me for
sympathy with his green eyes, his hair thinning,
midafternoon five o'clock shadow, blue uniform
shirtsleeves rolled up above the elbow revealing
thin hairy arms, mole on the inside of his left
forearm like a big period at the end of a tattoo
that reads MAMMA TU SOFFERTO PER MI. How much
did he charge you for the cream he asks and I tell
him and he shakes his head you could get it for
five cents less anywhere else.

SATURDAY SEASON'S FIRST snowstorm predicted for
Sunday everyone looking to get their snow tires
put on Joe and I change tires nine hours straight
stopping only for a quick sub around noon. Not

allowed to use the power wrench when we change tires my father says they strip the lugs which they don't we do it all by hand with lug wrenches by the end of the day my arms ache. Some snow tires already mounted on rims we loosen the lug nuts, jack up the rear end of the car, spin the lugs off, remove the tire and replace it with the snow tread, spin the lugs back on snug, drop the car back down, tighten the lugs, pop the hubcap on and we're through. Other snow tires aren't mounted on rims so when we get the summer tires off we must remove them from their rims on a machine bolted to the concrete floor. The machine holds the tire tight while I get under the lip of the tire with a bar turn the bar round till the tire lip's off do the same to the bottom then put the snow tread on reversing the procedure. Sometimes I have trouble mounting a snow tire since over the summer its rubber has dried or gone out of shape being stored incorrectly in someone's garage or basement floor. Then I spray it with rubber lube really bend and bang the bar to get the tire mounted and if I can't get it to inflate and seal properly around the rim which often happens with brand-new tires or tires that haven't been stored properly, I place an air belt around it which inflates squeezes the tire from the center more banging and pulling it will catch if not I call Blackie over he bangs and readjusts the belt swears Jesus Fucking Christ or come on you motherfucker bangs and eventually the tire catches. We bang and jack 'em up and let the jack down by end of day how many sets snow tires. My father gives us a wad of cash to split more than a hundred dollars at two dollars per set of tires four dollars if they're not mounted over fifty dollars each first time the old man's ever paid me for a day's work must have won big at the track.

THE AMBULANCE DEPARTS siren wails as we arrive State Police have closed off the lane, red, orange, blue, pink colored lights flash and swirl from police cruisers, tow truck and road flares, a light show in the dark into which my father and I rush turning the colors of our faces and blue uniforms yellows orange crazy pinks purple. Scratchy voices blare from police radios Volkswagen Bug's run into a concrete bridge pillar front half of the

Volkswagen wrapped around the pillar cars and trucks ripping by in the other lanes inside on the driver's side floor lone penny loafer caught in gnarled metal pool of blood on floor front seat dashboard splattered I can't breathe my father yells let's get going back to the tow truck dig hooks and chains out from the wooden red box first push the Volkswagen off from the pillar too wrecked to tow from the rear but we can't push Volkswagen off it's infused with the pillar so down on my back under the Volkswagen with flashlight look for a place to hook so we can first pull the car off the pillar with the truck then hook it and tow it away from its demolished front. I ask a trooper if the driver's dead says he was still alive when they took him away finally get the car off of the pillar then get it winched from the front a car pulls up a woman climbs out of the passenger side hysterical shrill-screams that's my son's car that's my son's car that's my son's car. The officers approach her and guide her back that's my son's car she's back in the car with the windows closed I can hear her glass-muffled screams that's my son's car. Every day I go out back look into the Volkswagen various color stages blood early bright red to livery brown I dream I try the penny loafer on looks very big but fits fine I'm working but it isn't really at the station my friend Jerry Hastings is here to inspect the wreck after school the driver's alive and after several months of intense recovery and therapy appears one afternoon to pay the bill on the Volkswagen and sign release papers for us to junk the totaled vehicle. It's been weeks since I've looked inside but when Spadafora the junk man comes to tow it away one last look tarry brown bloodstains shards of broken glass penny loafer tangled in twisted metal that's my son's car.

TINY'S GOT THE best flattop haircut works for my father during the fifties big bruiser-type guy but gentle and quiet works Saturdays now a day or two during the week if busy he's got cancer a hole in his throat covered by a white cotton bandage scratchy voice a great effort for him to talk clumsy often drops things smokes Luckies though he shouldn't smoke with his cancer drinks ice-cold bottles Pepsi down five or six gulps huge lunches of steak bombs veal cutlet subs large french fries the old man buys lunch for the crew says Tiny could put him out of business. Tiny punctures a hole in the radiator replacing a water pump on a '60 Plymouth Belvedere hands me a quarter go down the Jew's buy a bunch of Juicy Fruit gum when Harry comes down he tells me *his* version I say people are funny that way Tiny and I chew up several packs of Juicy Fruit which he plugs the radiator hole with don't say anything to the old man I won't. My father looks at the clock says take Countess up to the pond for a bath wants to get rid of me hear him on the phone today talking low making some kind of plans been a long, slow, hot day many pond visitors packing up or already gone strange silent humdrum heat-haze brush Countess her day's clumps loose hair let go her collar she dives straight in swims a large sweeping circle returns right back to me drenched shakes water off soaks me lather her up with shampoo back she goes take off my Oak St. Jenney shirt socks and shoes go in with blue jeans water's still clear cool swim out sandy bottom copper-yellow late afternoon sun hue slants ten or twelve feet below. Countess excited swims

near too close get my arms scratched by her dog-
paddling claws slowly tread water in the middle
of the pond onshore lifeguards turn over the row-
boat pull in barrel markers late sun orange-gold
band head to toe to bottom sand.

JOE AND RED alternate their drinking so one of
them takes care of their mother. Red returns home
from a weeklong bender Joe's been dry about two
weeks hanging around making some cash polish-
ing cars last couple of days says he's thirsting for
a cool one he talks about it for a few days sonny
I'm thirsting for a cool one then disappears for
three days returns sick for the rest of the week
his ulcer. Sometimes he goes out with Annie but
not really going out they just go somewhere and
fuck like Annie and George though George takes
her out somewhere in his Oldsmobile 98 the pond
at night they do it there. Joe takes her out to the
rear garage the old man keeps padlocked cars in
storage they do it inside one of the cars. Tommy
swears he and Annie haven't done it Joe and
George say he has Tommy says they shouldn't kid

around like that 'cause if his wife ever catches wind she'll have his balls. They sound disgusted when they talk about Annie like they don't like her or like fucking her. She's kind of heavy bad facial skin stories I hear she really likes getting it sometimes I think of her when I masturbate doesn't work out. Joe only goes with her if he's drinking sober swears he'll never go near her again neither Joe nor Red ever married Joe talks a lot about a Puerto Rican woman Maria he was in love with worked as a maintenance man at Boston College she's a cleaning woman in one of the dorms how they do it in a broom closet hear students walking by in the hall tiniest prettiest little quiffer he illustrates with his fingers delicate oblong shape one hot day both drenched with sweat in the broom closet I wonder whatever happened to my Maria. Joe says Tommy's definitely fucking Annie but doesn't want anyone to know. Tommy works three nights a week sometimes Saturdays during the day he works at a parts store fancies himself a mechanic mostly pumps gas his friend George hangs out with him sometimes Tommy'll do some minor work like a tune-up uses Chilton auto repair manuals to make sure he's got plugs

and points set right timing mark correctly marked
sure sign says Blackie of someone who doesn't
know what the fuck they're doing's when they use
a manual for something simple as a tune-up.
Tommy's a dark, big, roly-poly guy eats three and
four donuts at a time with Pepsi old man says he
steals laziest guy who's ever worked for him.
Tommy moves slow does little when I'm hanging around has me pump gas unless it's a woman
driver 'cause now so many of them are wearing
miniskirts all of the guys, Tommy, Joe, Blackie,
George, Phil, even my father, rush out to the pump
island to wash the windshield whenever a woman
pulls in race among themselves see who gets there
first only time Tommy's in any hurry. Tommy says
true sign of a guy hasn't got a fucking clue about
broads says I love you when he's fucking one.

SCHOOL'S OUT HE'S waiting for me out front in the
tow truck no time for a cigarette Jerry Hastings
hands me off a couple which I pocket and hop in
the truck. Everyone comes at the last minute for
inspection folks who've been holding back they

know something's wrong with their cars we write lots of rejection stickers pick up much repair work the last week of the season. I help Blackie in the garage checking registration numbers, brake lights and directionals, scraping old stickers off, replacing taillight bulbs, headlights, flasher fuses. Traffic's backing up on the street waiting line old man's out there directing whistling broken English yelling to folks bring it arounda put it ovah deer hey pull it uppa pull it uppa. Those rejected argue a ball joint isn't loose or a bald tire's legal, but nobody wins an argument with my father. Anyone gives Blackie a hard time he calls the old man who pulls out the book shoves it in faces goes on like this for hours until around 7:00 when Blackie leaves. My mother brings big bowls macaroni meatballs and sausages. Around 7:30 he takes off okay with me I've got homework to do which I half-do between the trickle of gas customers and assorted visitors. A '64 Ford comes in and pulls up to the air pump on the side of the building. The driver gets out takes the hose off the lever but I don't hear any air pumping. I look out the door 'round the corner he picks up the hose I've startled him looks like he's been nosing around

out back. Got a tire gauge he asks one right on
the pump I tell him oh yeah didn't see it he checks
the air on his left front tire thanks me leaves the
hose on the ground backs out and drives away.
Two years every day at school Kathy Quinlan tells
me she sees my father the night before at her house
what's he doing at her house visiting her mother?
Don't see her much since I've been in high school
he's probably down Wonderland chasing the dogs
he was penciling around the race form while he
ate. Around quarter to nine Annie pulls in with
her 1965 red Ford Mustang convertible glows
under huge overhead pump island lights. Fill it
up I remain in the rear hold off washing her windshield avoid conversation with her only takes
three gallons backs up throws gas over the bumper
and my pants. Wash the bumper with water collect money aren't you going to do my windshield?
Oh sure I forgot grab the squeegee start on passenger side over to her side anybody around?
Freddy Golar was here earlier. Joe too. George?
No haven't seen George probably tomorrow night
when Tommy works. Thanks sweetie she says
leaves in a flash peels out her tires faint hint of
rubber smell in air.

WORKING UNDER CARS winter snow and ice forms under wheel wells, on bumpers, in corners of chassis and frames. Once a car's up on the lift starts melting rain of ice-cold drops down my back on my head all day long every day for months cold water soaking my hair slush down my neck into my eyes. Joe's drunk singing "Prince Edward Island" the old man heads out for lunch returns two large pizzas one pepperoni the other sausage Blackie takes the cheese, pepperoni, and sausage off and gives it to me. The old man tries to get Joe to eat a slice pizza into the Pepsi machine pulls out last can of beer from his six-pack. John the postman comes to collect for the number — John's numbers racket brings him more money than his mailman job the old man's been playing a number given to him by my grandfather in a dream always says things like Grandpa came to me in a dream last night told me play this number or that horse. Blackie plays the same number every day for years a dime a day he's hit three or four times. If I want to play a number I've got to do it through Joe the old man would flip if he found out I'm gambling but Joe's been drinking all morning too drunk and silly to communicate with. My father says this is what happens with Joe soon as he works a few days cleaned and polished a few cars, he's got some money in his pocket and off he goes. Joe leaves when his beer's gone won't see him for a week or so rest of afternoon is slow the old man takes off, Blackie does a little maintenance work on the tow truck. I'm sitting in the office listening to WRKO, watching the clock hands slip second by second, minute by minute away on the old dirty illuminated B. F. Goodrich clock. An occasional gas customer, Beatles on the radio, fierce battle in Viet Nam, where is Viet Nam how do you say it right, kids returning from the pond dripping swimsuits and hair, who needs a dime for the bus.

MY FATHER GRABS Countess by her collar left hand a crowbar raised in his right says now get the fuck out of here the Jehovah's Witness guy turns and flees reaches the curb opposite side of the street turns and glares my father stands this side of the street crowbar in one hand Countess in the other stay the fuck out of here now. He comes around to pass out literature friendly anyone ever wonder what a Jehovah's Witness is everyone says no my father not interested then Red says yeah I've wondered what a Jehovah's Witness is the man proceeds to take Red aside very seriously talks about what being a Jehovah's Witness means Red listens nods yeah after five minutes the old man says okay that's enough but the man's persistent and Red's acting goofy looks at me and Blackie grins the old man says okay we've got work to do but the man continues standing over Red who's in a chair finally the old man says look we're not interested in Jehovah's Witnesses we're Catholic. I've never seen him go to church but every now and then Father Everheart gasses up corners my father in the office asks us to leave and with the old man down on his knees without an argument Father Everheart hears his confession. For a few moments the man's determined states that Red wants to hear the word the old man says he's only kidding he doesn't want to be a fucking Jehovah's Witness Red looks up says yes I do I do want to be a Jehovah's Witness the old man says c'mon now Red enough is enough tells the guy get off my property the Jehovah's Witness says you can't stop me from spreading the word oh no my father wants to know gets the crowbar and Countess chases the Jehovah's Witness off. What are Jehovah's Witnesses I ask no one seems to know Red says they're pretty fucking weird though they don't eat meat and stuff like that but are they Christians. No they're not Christians my father says more like Jews.

"UNDER THE BOARDWALK" the Drifters? heat waves lift off station lot's asphalt my father off somewhere Blackie doesn't work Mondays during summer, Countess curled up in a cool corner of the garage too hot for her behind the station afternoon sun beats down back there. I rinse my head in the water trough my T-shirt cut off at the shoulders drenched with water and sweat haven't had a gas customer for over an hour watch the clock slow motion. Distant sirens closer make their way up the hill flash of ambulance and fire trucks pass I saw them turn in to the pond the lady in the '65 Plymouth Valiant says as I wash her windshield no sooner she pulls out first kids

start trickling down from the pond excited someone just drowned a girl. No not a girl it's a boy
it's one of the kids from Harris Park not one of
the kids from Harris Park it's one of the Mackey
kids not the Mackey kids I said hi to them this
morning when they walked by Frankie the second oldest thirteen cramps not cramps tangled
in weeds off Pickerel Rock. Pickerel Rock other
side of the pond no swimming allowed out of sight
of lifeguards ten-foot-high rock kids dive off.
Several people drown there over the years Frankie
Mackey hit his head on the rock diving his brothers jump in try pushing him up Maureen the oldest
stands on the rock has his hands in hers for minutes but can't pull him out too steep and the
water's too deep all the time Frankie's out cold
Shorty Monahan says right before Frankie dives
he takes off his Saint Christopher's medal gives
it to his brother Michael says here take my Saint
Christopher's medal for me in case something
happens. Shorty says all the Mackeys are going
crazy up there Michael's screaming Frankie
Frankie Frankie places the Saint Christopher's
medal around Frankie's neck when they have him
onshore ambulance drivers have to walk halfway

around the pond with their equipment and
stretcher 'cause there's no road for the ambulance
and when they get there Frankie's already dead
they try to revive him but can't so they put him
on the stretcher and at a trot take him out followed by all the screaming Mackeys and other
bystanders he'll be okay once they get him to the
hospital but everyone knows he's dead Shorty
says. Drowning's in the newspaper and locals are
outraged asking why kids are allowed to swim
there and I saw Mrs. Mackey and Mr. Mackey
drive by our house the morning of the funeral in
the black limousine looking straight ahead dazed.
The weather's hot for a couple of days foot traffic
to the pond is light though Shorty Monahan
still swims every day stops to talk says he still
can't believe it how Frankie removed his Saint
Christopher's medal gives it to his brother Michael
take my Saint Christopher's medal in case something happens.

I'M WEARING MY green Quaker State motor oil cap
big anniversary sale eight years old just learned

to pump gas Joe dressed as a clown hands balloons out to kids when he needs more fills them up with a big tank Al Moran the mechanic goes to the tank breathes in gas talks funny high-pitched cartoon voice. A huge mechanical cowboy robot out on sidewalk waves at drivers as they pass red white and blue flags flap everywhere in wind above the pump island strung out across the station lot on rope. Tire promotion dozens of tires strewn around the lot in multicolor ribboned B. F. Goodrich stands we're giving away drinking glasses with every purchase of five gallons or more sales representatives from Jenney and B. F. Goodrich walk around smiling and talking with customers. Bill Gleason from Jenney's a large man with white hair and red face always happy in various stages of drunkenness does many favors for my father like getting Jenney to paint the station before the big sale my father brings him home and my mother cooks for him he loves Italian food my mother runs around the kitchen in a simple blue and white check dress and her cooking apron, long straight brown hair brushed back in a ponytail, cooks and serves them pasta pizza soups and Bill eats one course after another all the time drinking whiskey and water telling my mother what an amazing woman she is getting up wrapping his arms around her thin five-foot-tall frame kisses her on the cheek how my father doesn't know how much of a good thing he's got she turns red my father sits smiles like it's entertainment. My sister laughs at his antics Bill squeezes her cheeks bella bella bella she pulls away turns to me motions turning her index finger to her head she thinks he's crazy. Bill eats and eats when he's finished into the cabinet for anisette a couple of glasses of anisette before he and my father leave wraps his bearlike arms around my mother again kisses her what an amazing woman you are running around making jokes everyone's laughing at inside the office has a shot of whiskey. Gilbert Jones B. F. Goodrich representative is a short balding white-haired man wears plaid sport jackets skinny bow ties white shoes smokes long menthol cigarettes when he lights one and takes that first drag his nostrils flair for some reason he reminds me of someone who's from the south though I don't know anyone from the south. Gilbert Jones buzzes around talks to customers explains specifics of new tire treads on B. F.

Goodrich tires why they are superior to all others why now's the time to buy prices never this low again. The anniversary sale goes on for three days each one of the days my mother brings huge pots of macaroni meatballs and sausages for everyone to eat for lunch. My father wins a portable black and white television for selling so many tires a photographer from the *Mercury* comes to take his photograph as he is presented the television by Gilbert Jones from B. F. Goodrich which the *Mercury* runs on the fifth page in their "Goings On About the Town" section my father still thin, hair thinning, smiling, bow-tied Gilbert Jones to my father's right in his green plaid sport coat which is black and white in the photo smiling as he hands my father the television and Al Moran standing on my father's left flattop haircut. Al Moran whose brother dies in an automobile accident on Interstate 93 driving north in the southbound lane runs straight into a tractor-trailer truck. My father frames the photo hangs it on the office wall next to the framed scratchy black and white photo of him on a hunting trip biting into one end of a foot-long submarine sandwich his friend Vinny Luongo biting the other between them hangs a big gutted dead deer Vinny shot inside cavity held wide open with heavy sticks.

MORNINGS PASS QUICKLY afternoons, if business is slow, drag. My father's at Rockingham catch a couple races Blackie's gone out for a couple of beers I listen to the radio, smoke cigarettes, wait on gas customers in the desk drawer girlie magazines. In the compressor room pinups takes a while interrupted by gas customers wait a minute until my dick softens before I go out the customer leaves back in start over. Delays don't bother me pleasurably prolong help pass the time leave the door open a crack see anyone driving in convinced the dark-haired woman with pigtails in pinup *not* Sally Field. Woman in pinups prettier than woman in magazines where people have sex skinnier acne nudist magazines don't entice bunch of naked people playing volleyball or tennis or eating barbecue puts me off they're older wrinkly but look to be enjoying themselves. I cum wipe with a rag roll it up place bottom of oil- and grime-soaked rag bin laundry company picks up each week replaces dirty orange-pink rags with bright clean pressed stack of rags, imagine someone at laundry company unfolding my cum-laced rag. Cold bottle of Pepsi, cigarette, check clock how much time killed.

TWO WEEKS AFTER half of Malden Square burns down my father takes me to the shoe store in Malden Square first pair work shoes real black steel-toe mechanic's shoes my feet finally big enough. The day of the fire droves of sirens every direction customer says Malden Square's burning down climb to roof of station in distance tips of flames waves of rising black smoke. Next day local television news shows reels of buildings burning front page *Record American* runs a half-page color photo old Strand Theatre ablaze. First chance see damage myself shoe store my father buys work shoes from didn't get touched had the wind not died down when it did the fire would have swallowed up the entire square. Up the stairs we climb third floor three-floor red-brick building amid a whole block three- and four-story red-bricks three blocks away from last block the fire destroyed. Burned out gutted buildings still stand windows boarded yellow ribbon fences run lengths of blocks keep out danger signs every twenty or thirty feet. The Strand Theatre and one of the old factories long since closed collapsed all's left piles red bricks and burned-black timbers twisted wreckage of the Strand Theatre marquee. Little shoe store not like most shoe stores with fancy displays woman who owns the place my father knows buys work shoes here for years sizes me up you've got small feet. I want to know about the fire she obliges with minute-by-minute account what happens day of fire points out you can still smell smoke and I do describes how she first hears the old Parker Building's burning on Pleasant Street a little while later fire spreads down the block soon news the Strand Theatre's burning and finally she closes the store to investigate the Strand Theatre is fully engulfed in flames wind blowing firemen being called from neighboring cities to help contain spreading flames within the block but by early afternoon windblown flames ignite other buildings and blocks other side of the square the building her store's in out of danger she returns opens up again within an hour another block succumbs others in her building growing restless around three in the afternoon black smoke permeates hallways and shops fire burning its way closer and closer then the fireman came up and told us all to leave the building. Then the firemen came up and told us all to leave the building. Something about the way she delivers that line the sounds of her words as if she's in a play then the firemen came up and told us all to leave the building same way Lenny Barns and his story of the gas station fire over time retelling the story so it sounds better with each telling then the firemen came up and told us all to leave the building. Everyone in the building evacuates but the wind's lessening fire's coming under control only a few blocks from the shoe store by early evening her building's out of danger. At home in bed new black work shoes on floor can't sleep can't wait to wear my shoes to the station tomorrow, turn her words over. Days, weeks, months her words in my mind my mouth mouthing the sentence then the firemen came up and told us all to leave the building.

BLACKIE REPAIRS FOREIGN cars more of them around these days extra business most local mechanics don't own metric tools or know anything about Volkswagens or Triumphs or Fiats popular with long-haired college students from Harvard and Tufts. Blackie's pulling the engine from an MG Midget help him slide it over and away from the car methodically proceed to dismantle it. I remove intake and exhaust manifolds hoses and anything hanging loose Blackie points out gunked-up rocker arm assembly from oil not being changed enough that's why the engine spun a bearing in the first place. He takes off the rocker arm assembly unbolts the head bolts we lift off the head valves are beat Blackie wonders how the number three fired at all raise the engine block higher in the air with the pulley I remove the oil pan Blackie lets me unbolt the crankcase bolts which hold the piston rod bearings wrapped around the crankcase at number three cylinder bearing cap fragments of spun bearing fall into my hands I knew it Blackie says. Remove bearing caps, pop the rods up, pull the pistons out number three piston's leaking piston rings are shot so it goes until we've a complete dismantled engine —

rocker arm assembly, lifters, pistons, rods, crankcase valves intake manifold exhaust manifold belts
hoses water pump fan timing chain carburetor
block head hundreds nuts and bolts strewn over
the garage floor. I organize parts nuts and bolts
into boxes so we can find them when time to put
it back together after the head's rebuilt with new
valves and the crankcase ground down new rings
replaced heads of pistons wire-brushed and buffed
I spend a half day scraping gunk off other parts
sanding down gasket areas so new gaskets hold
tight without leaks. Blackie knows all the ins and
outs be careful not to overbore the block or the
pistons won't fit back right and lube new bearings with STP before you replace 'em to avoid
metal to metal friction when the engine's all back
together and started and use the torque wrench
every key nut and bolt from crankcase bearings
to head bolts has torque specification must be
tightened exactly to specification with the torque
wrench effortlessly one task to another occasion-
ally stuck Blackie swears come on you motherfucker or Jesus fucking Christ until he works it
through. I'm smoking Blackie's Pall Malls radio
tuned to Blackie's oldies station in between shop-

talk Blackie talks about girls and parties when he was a biker and his old '49 Ford if he had a dime for every time he got laid in that car. Moment of fate rebuilt engine's lowered back into a car, buttoned up to its transmission, exhaust system, bolted down to the motor mounts — hoses, belts, fuel lines, water lines and linkages connected up and Blackie instructs me get in and turn it over. They never start on first turn usually the distributor's not in quite right timing's off or the carburetor needs adjusting once a Triumph Spitfire did turn right over and we couldn't believe it but ten minutes running seized up and a half day fiddling Blackie says the engine's got to come out again turns out parts store sent the wrong bearings even though they fit when he placed them in and bolted them down but once the engine started they gave in so he begins the procedure over again my father fights to get the parts store guys to admit it was their fault and assume the cost of tearing the engine apart a second time. When it's all done listening to it run hard to believe that fucker was sitting on the floor in a thousand pieces two days ago Blackie says purring like a fucking kitten now.

PARTS STORE BONANZA discount oil filters my father buys them up runs a special lube oil and filter lowest price around regular and new customers take advantage. I know all our regular customers by name, quickest way to find out where strangers get their cars serviced is look on the inside driver's door thin sticker name of service center date of last service performed, odometer reading, services performed. I tear them off replace with new interesting how long people go between oil changes should be every two thousand miles most go way beyond and many don't change the oil filter when they change the oil Blackie says like washing your face with dirty water because the filter's where all grime from the oil system ends up so clean oil runs through a dirty filter. Oil filters must be tightened by hand if tightened too tight gaskets strip and leak and if an oil filter hasn't been changed in a long time it's extremely difficult to remove must use a tool that's a handle with a belt band attached wrap the belt band around the filter tighten it up then turn the handle. Sometimes they still won't budge Blackie says last Mickey Mouse mechanic put it on too tight he takes a long screwdriver with a hammer

bangs it straight through dirty oil splatters everywhere including my hair once the filter's drained
turn the big screwdriver the filter turns off with
it. Several weeks lube oil and filter business booms
big sign out front LUBE OIL AND FILTER BONANZA.
When the first of the BONANZA cars returns with
a leaky filter my father blames me put it on too
tight stripped the gaskets but first thing I learn
about replacing an oil filter is to tighten it by hand
so we replace it and when more cars return Blackie
begins to suspect the filters faulty over half the
cars come back with leaks and my father calls
other stations same problems he calls Sammy at
the parts store Sammy I've got news for you your
BONANZA KAPUTZ!

POUR LAST OF the hot chocolate from red and black
plaid thermos brought by my mother into red
plastic cup. Lukewarm. Two degrees outside wind
gusts who knows how cold dressed in layers take
off outer coat inside between customers. Mittens
do fine but hard to make change or write credit
card slip take them off put in jacket pockets my

hands dried and cracked. No one out tonight Oak Street like a quiet country road smoke seven cigarettes masturbate maybe Joe'll come down what's going on with Annie she likes George really wants to date you Tommy says to him George has a nine-inch dick this is what she wants George says grabbing himself Joe says she's really good and likes to get it. George says she's too ugly Tommy says it's not the face you fuck but the fuck you face. Fiercest rain or snowstorm or coldest day of year's when people decide they need their oil or tire pressure checked driving rain down a quart put one in the lady says 55¢ 65¢ or 90¢. 65¢. I put it in she pays me a dime short I say you're a dime short she says 55¢ for the oil I put in the 65¢ 'cause that's what you said I told you 55¢ she insists and I'm standing in downpour getting drenched my father comes out what's going on I tell him he takes a dime out his pocket gives it to her says here's your goddamn dime don't come back keeping the kid out here in pouring rain. Hydraulic systems art forms in themselves jack up a '62 Cadillac four door bumper jack lifts whole half car all because a little piston and petroleum mix in a valve and ring-sealed unit. Floor jacks smaller for jacking one quarter of the car up least safe of jacks, bumper jacks have safety bolts steadier easier for a car to slip off a floor jack especially if either the car or the floor jack is bumped. Lots of guys have stories about the time the jack slipped my father knows a guy killed under a car in a jack accident if you're going to get under a car for long you jack it up and onto jack stands. On the pumps the numbers tumble click-clocking the amount of gas pumped the amount of cash owed. Every six months an official comes around tests the pumps makes certain amount of gas pumped is consistent with amount owed otherwise what would prevent gas sellers from fixing pump mechanisms to their own advantage. At the same time a sample of regular and premium is taken sent to a lab tested to make certain 87 octane actually 87 octane and the 90 octane 90 octane. The new pumps sleeker and angular old ones taller thinner and round at the top. We're one of the last to get new chrome pumps I polish every two weeks old pumps peeling faded metal paint red. We pump 500 to 1,000 gallons of gas a day barely pays the rent real profits from repair work and inspection time or special events like tire or battery sales. My father gives my mother $100 a week some days we make more than that in repairs alone he loses a lot at the track some months he's behind on bills even when it's busy. I love the smell of gasoline instant I begin to pump first delicious waves tickle and burn my nostrils swear I could drink it.

I MAKE DIME phone calls for a nickel Blackie shows me to how drop a nickel in the hole and just when it falls through the mechanism it clicks right then pop the coin return button with the palm of my hand a dial tone. Timing's everything. Months of practice I don't believe it can be done except Blackie does it all the time finally I get a dial tone a dozen more tries before I do it again then every fourth time every second now any time on any pay phone for a nickel I can call. Blackie knows these little tricks drives a standard can shift through all four gears without using a clutch in the tow truck watch him gently push his way through all four never a hint of a gear grinding. I've tried several times no luck afraid of trans-

mission damage, my father says it can't be done
he's seen Blackie do it insists it damages the transmission Blackie says you don't know the first thing
about transmissions and he doesn't. My father
can't make phone calls for a nickel tried many
times when he needs to make a phone call he has
me or Blackie get a dial tone for him. The guys
at the parts store like to give my father a hard
time they know he's hotheaded stubborn and
won't order his parts from Gus Sammy's partner
because Gus always screws up orders so he calls
asks for Sammy even when Gus answers sometimes Gus lets the phone sit on the counter doesn't
tell Sammy my father says he can hear them all
talking and he starts whistling into the phone
yelling S-A-M-M-Y everyone at the parts store
gets a laugh listening. I'm not aware of my father's
accent until I hear him converse with others and
realize they have a difficult time understanding
him he shouts into the phone I got a business to
run and this is not funny Gus comes out *I'g abusin
ta run and isa no fungus* or he orders me to *take-
u de fron ties offa da blue Buke and balanca.*
We're out on Interstate 93 south near the 128
intersection heavy traffic whips dangerously close

by pick a '61 Chevy Impala up by the front end ready to tow away a car pulls up behind us horn blowing a guy gets out passenger side yells stop. His '61 Chevy Impala's out of gas he's got a canful my father says that's fine but still going to have to pay him for the tow 'cause we were called by the State Police already have the car on back of tow truck but the guy says no way he's going to pay he left a note in the window that he was out of gas and the State Police had no right to call my father who says yes they do you can't aban- don a car in the breakdown lane says so on all the signs on the entry ramps but the man insists my father let the car down off the tow truck boom my father says not until you pay $15 for the tow guy says you haven't towed it anywhere soon as it's up on the boom it's a tow and even if it wasn't you have to pay for the road service guy says he didn't call for road service my father says pay for the tow now or we'll tow it and once it's in the station I'll charge you a day's storage charge guy says I order you to put the car down now my father says no way I'll see you at the station the guy threatens to sue you'll be walking to your lawyer's office. The man offers to pay $10 my father says okay the man pays the ten I let the car down off the boom unhook the chains and free the '61 Chevy — we're getting in the tow truck the guy's pouring gas into his car yells now I know what highway robbery is my father says now I know what an asshole is in the tow truck he adds if the guy wasn't such an asshole he would have told him $10 right from the start.

BLACKIE STANDS OVER his '55 Chevy, hood open, large Styrofoam cup full of coffee in left hand, freshly lit Pall Mall in right, stares into that 283 quietly humming red rag hangs out right rear pocket of his blue uniform pants, open-end wrench sticks out the left. Someone always drops by with half dozen and coffee mine small cream extra sugar Blackie large regular my father small regular Joe black no sugar Tommy large milk George small cream no sugar Floyd large black with sugar. Floyd works Sundays and Saturdays if it's busy on Saturdays he gets a ride from his girlfriend but on Sundays my father picks him up takes him home after closing. Floyd doesn't have

a license alcoholic my father makes me ring the
bell at the beat-up three-decker Floyd lives in in
Chelsea. He doesn't answer means he's been
drinking down the street to a pay phone my father rings him after several minutes Floyd picks
up the phone I'm always fearful he won't means
I've got to pull the Sunday shift. Floyd's a short
solid man with marble green eyes, greased back
dark hair, sideburns and a long bone-carved nose
which has a bump from being broken he got into
trouble when younger spent time in jail but my
father says you can trust Floyd though he makes
mistakes and has accidents drops the charge card
machine on glass desktop or pours a quart of oil
into someone's radiator. The guy who works Sundays before Floyd sells his own oil out the trunk
of his car my father can't figure out why he doesn't
sell oil on Sundays finally gets on to the guy and
fires him. Except on busiest days there's time to
take ten have a honey dipped coffee and cigarette
and in the process we end up standing around
looking at and discussing a car — Phil's Corvette,
George's big black brand-new Oldsmobile 98,
Joe's brand-new 1965 Chevy Impala red with
black vinyl roof red interior two-door 283 V-8,

GAS STATION

Tommy's green '62 Buick Tommy will only own
Buicks, Billy Zona's '54 Ford coupe, Blackie's '55
Chevy Bel Air. Blackie's forever fiddling with that
283 runs so perfectly strain to hear it like an
antisound. I do legwork when my father and I
plow, most driveways straightforward a few have
some bends the plow can't get at I'm out there
with a shovel then ring doorbells to collect money
he remains warm and dry in the old Willys. Ten
dollars a driveway plow a dozen or so every storm
works out for the old man because the storms
bring school cancellations he gets me for the day.
I think my father's been with Annie too, something about the way they're talking, kind of
flirting, she brings coffee in the afternoons even
though she knows George isn't here hangs out in
the office talks with my father. Blackie loses tools
a lot swears where the fuck did I put that usually a wrench or pair of pliers finds in his back
pocket or under some parts he's removed and
placed down somewhere. It's real cold road service calls people with dead batteries need a jump
battery charger runs all day line of batteries waiting to be recharged. I don't like working with
batteries acid forms around the cables and posts

burns layers of skin on my hands a guy who got battery acid in his eyes went blind. My father does work free for Tom Riordan who needs a jump my father rushes right over to his house no matter how many calls are ahead we plow Tom Riordan's driveway for nothing my father says he can't put a dollar value on all the favors Tom's done for him. I'm carrying a battery by a battery strap which holds the battery by its posts one end slips off battery falls to ground narrowly missing my foot it could have crushed a corner breaks makes terrible mess acid burns a stain on the hot top.

GREASING A CAR rainy or snowy days water drips everywhere down my back reach with my hand to find grease fittings upper ball joints then lower ball joints two fittings on the tie-rod assembly one on the driveshaft. I squeeze too much grease into a fitting blob of grease lands on my shoulder wipe the glob off with a rag. If a car's front end's not greased frequently ball joints or tie-rods will dry out causing metal-to-metal friction. 1962 Ford

Falcon we tow from Interstate 93 tie-rod assembly snapped right front tire caves in Falcon skids across three lanes and down a steep embankment. Traffic's light my father says if it happened during rush hour there'd be a major pileup. Johnny Whittier can't use his arms polio when he was a kid a contraption on his 1964 Ford Galaxie 500 allows him to drive and steer with his feet, he places his right foot into a wheel on the floor to steer while he controls gas and brake with his left foot. The electrical system switches — wipers, horn, lights — transmission shifting, opening and closing doors are all worked with his feet and knees. In 1958 he buys a brand-new Ford and a mechanic at Ford rigs Johnny's first car it's never quite right things break down frequently and his accessibility to the electrical system switches is limited. Blackie studies the job the Ford mechanic did so when Johnny buys another new car Blackie does a better job designing and building the special assembly than people at Ford. Several weeks Blackie works on Johnny's new Ford, takes trips back and forth to machine shops for parts and pieces he's designed to be made to specifications. There's only a half a dozen cars like Johnny's in

the country I watch him drive arms and hands
limp by his sides, fingers limply folded into palms,
legs and knees turning and bumping, starting and
stopping, wants a Pepsi I hold under his chin the
bottle while he sips through a straw he has lunch
with us after I'm finished with my sub cut his up
into small pieces and feed him his ham and cheese.
Johnny runs the concession stand at the pond
winters in Florida his girlfriend actually does most
of the work and he oversees she's younger than
he is though Johnny's a fuckhound Joe says he's
got a second woman on the side I wonder how
Johnny fucks must be on his back with her on
top greasing his '64 Ford is tricky because of all
the extra fittings in the special assembly he stands
around watches over me points with his forehead
you missed one there.

BILL GLEASON DRINKS Little Nicks at the kitchen
table finishes his second bowl of macaroni what
a fantastic cook my mother smiles fries veal cut-
lets at the stove serves them with fresh tomato
sauce and salad from greens I pick from the gar-

den. Mamma mia Bill says kisses tips of his fingers like he thinks Italians do you've outdone yourself again my father tells my sister get Bill another bottle of beer she says no he raises his eyebrows and his voice what did I just tell you and she goes to the refrigerator brings Bill his beer he reaches for her cheek bella donna she pulls away my father grinds his jaw gives her a look of rage she settles down. He turns to Bill what about the paint job Bill throws his fork down mamma mia do you have to start now I told you don't worry you're going to getta da paint mimics my father my father doesn't own the gas station he's a proprietor responsible for regular maintenance while services like painting are performed by the Jenney Company but Jenney neglects us low gas volume outside paint's peeling and yellowing. Bill tells my father before the end of summer he'll have a fresh coat of paint on the walls relax you worry too much his face turns redder the more he eats and drinks he's already half drunk when he arrives near suppertime which means he's looking for my father to take him home for food. After he eats he helps himself to the liqueur cabinet pours copious amounts of

anisette into his black coffee another terrific meal
is he being good to you oh I guess so her shy smile
most of the time well he better be and if not you
let me know and I'll straighten him out.

MY FATHER'S FEET stink awful during the summer
sitting on his ass leaning back on his hands holding a tire stable with his two feet Blackie's on the
creeper working on the wheel bearings backs himself out from under the car says get the fuck away
from me with those things he can smell my father's
feet through his shoes. Sometimes in the afternoon
my father sits in the office, removes his shoes and
socks, places his feet directly in front of the fan
to cool them you could clear Fenway Park with
those things Joe says. I pull the tow truck to the
side of the building and wash it when I'm through
Blackie hands me keys to his Chevy lets me move
it over give it a wash. The old man's finally letting me drive again and allows me to drive to and
from home in the tow truck a few months ago
I'm moving a black 1963 Ford Galaxie away from
the pumps racing the engine by accident I pop the

automatic into reverse lay down some rubber right there tearing into it damn near run over the old man out of the way just in time swears and screams waves his arms I jam the brake screeching halt. He's pissed for days says I can't drive again until I have a license which is still two years away but Blackie still lets me move cars when the old man's out and when I run errands with Joe he lets me drive his car a few days ago I was moving the tow truck when the old man pulls in sees me not a word. First time I ever drive I'm ten grounded a bad report card he brings me to the station to pump gas on Saturdays comes home for supper with a car on the back of the tow truck to be towed to Spadafora's Junk in Malden before dinner he and my mother are arguing over money he hasn't been giving her enough. My sister and I are fighting at dinner we're kicking each other under table he and my mother eating in silence I let out a belch at my sister he swings a backhander across the table catches me on the side of the face says we eat and shut up inside of my cheek cut against my teeth taste blood in the tomato sauce start to cry but choke down my tears don't you start crying now. After supper I go to my room he sticks his head in come with me to drop a car off in Malden put on my shoes he's waiting for me in the truck. I know where all the gears are and how to use the clutch he's been promising to let me drive I sit in the truck when it's parked practice going through the gears. Spadafora's Junkyard is acres big row upon row of junk cars stacks of fenders rear ends engine blocks tires rims radiators bumpers doors long rows of shelves with windshields and windows a towering crane that can pick a car up and with one sweep transfer it to the crusher on the other side of the yard. Inside the office my father's talking to Spaddy wearing same grimed blue overalls every time I see him Jane's Fortune in the seventh he says to my father I'm telling you the dog can't miss all the time short cigar stub clenched between his teeth. Back in the tow truck he drives in the opposite direction where are we going to run an errand turning onto the Revere Beach Parkway follow it around Bell Circle slow down as we approach Wonderland take a right into the parking lot I'm going to be about fifteen minutes wait in the truck departing in a hurry and trotting across the parkway through the entrance gate. The

windows are rolled down and I can smell the
ocean and see the roller coaster off in the distance
at Revere Beach suddenly voracious roar of a
crowd coming from behind the high fence man's
voice over loudspeaker can't make out his words.
Rub my tongue against the fresh cut inside my
mouth get out of the truck walk across the parkway can't see over the fence look through narrow
space between fence slats lots of bright lights and
green another great crowd-roar loudspeaker voice
and there goes Swifty. Seems like an hour before
he returns drives to the far side of the lot which
is vacant stops asks you ready I want to know
for what he says to drive. The truck lurches forward then stalls I let the clutch out too quickly
slow he shouts let the clutch out slow three or
four more times before I'm able to move forward
shift it into second now I push the clutch in pull
the shifter toward second gears grind second second he yells screech to a halt it goes on this way
several more attempts until I'm able to take off
and shift properly into second gain enough speed
shift it into third around the vast parking lot about
ten minutes until he has me stop and back in
the driver's seat he drives out of the parking lot

toward home don't say anything to your mother about coming here. He does wash his feet regularly don't know why they're so rank his white socks permanently stained mustard yellow no matter how much my mother bleaches them.

CHRISTMAS EVE DAY people won't schedule any regular maintenance work only emergency Mrs. Bowlan's '60 Plymouth wagon exhaust system clamp snaps Fellsway Shopping Center parking lot three quarters of the exhaust system on the ground I'm under the Plymouth with wire a pair of wire cutters ice and slush my back is soaked tie up the exhaust best I can drive the wagon to the station replace the clamp back the car out of the garage the oil pan catches the corner of the lift not fully down tears a small hole in the oil pan oil leaks all over a gallon of the black stuff garage floor puddles the old man shouts soon as he finds out Blackie saves me says it's his fault he thought the lift was down told me to back it out brand-new oil pan's expensive from the Plymouth dealer my father calls Spaddy at Spadafora's Junk

they have one cheap he's still pissed because he
has to take the time to go pick it up and he can't
get to tending his annual office party sets a little
bar up strings some lights everyone gets offered
a drink there's eggnog he mixes with whiskey only
a few takers in the morning the mailman and Mr.
Laporta who drinks a lot his face red smell it on
his breath it's only nine thirty in the morning
happy holidays drinks a healthy shot down
Freddy Golar staggers in at eleven several belts
toasts everyone asks my father won't you have
one with me but my father doesn't drink first
Christmas we haven't sold Christmas trees out of
the station first week of December my father and
I drive up Route 1 towards the New Hampshire
border meet the truck packed full with trees down
from Maine driver follows us to the station drops
off the trees my father pays him cash each year
sell fewer and fewer trees last year lose money
too many people buy artificial trees this year he
bought one too.

IF YOU CAN beat me you can eat me read the

bumper sticker of a woman who used to hang out at the White Tower restaurant drove a 1957 Corvette convertible full-blown engine no one ever did beat her Blackie says that Corvette was so fucking fast Phil wants to know what ever happened to that spoiled little rich bitch. The White Tower on Broadway Somerville's a burger joint hangout for rodders and bikers Blackie says now it's mostly kids he hardly knows any of them. During the fifties there was much street drag racing Blackie and Phil remember a stretch of road on Route 2 near Concord measured off for a quarter of a mile late Saturday nights anyone who's anybody is there to race cars and bikes get laid and there's a flagman in the middle of the road waving the official start they race through the night down to final two the winner floats through the next week honors of being reigning champion can get any girl he wants except during that period of time none could beat this woman in the 1957 Corvette convertible *W - A - O - U - W* Phil says could that fucking Corvette fly *W - A - O - U - W* was she a looker too. Blackie says she married a guy with more money than her father had lives somewhere in the suburbs has kids and gets a new Cadillac every two years. Phil comes in late morning puffy half-mast eyes he's been out the night before drinking and partying with a woman you should have heard this broad screaming reenacts details of his date last night parking at the Sheepfold she was just dying for it and you should have heard this broad screaming give it to me give it to me I had to roll up the fucking windows. The Sheepfold on Route 28's part of the Middlesex Fells Reservation woods long time ago farmers grazed sheep and cattle there now it's used as a picnic area by day at night couples go parking once my friends and I go there find used discarded condoms on the ground. Phil's old to be parking he's old as Blackie and Tommy and Blackie and Tommy have kids. Phil still lives with his parents doesn't work not sure where his money comes from hangs around drives his Corvette to the beach or to clubs like Sammy's Patio down Revere Beach where he and Blackie know everyone. Blackie knows the woman Phil's talking about says I remember those screams well that's why they call her Screaming Laura. Man you ain't kidding one fucking bit Phil says, W - A - O - U - W.

HARD TO KEEP the men's room clean everybody uses it all day women's room around the side of the building keep locked gets little use clean it once a week wash the floor, sink, mirror and toilet it's already clean. Sometimes George or Tommy or Joe uses the women's room with Annie door locks from the inside tight in there not too tight for blow jobs though George fucked Annie in there standing up I can't imagine George so tall Annie short. Men's room's inside the office clean every day floor gets dirty sink and toilet too. He walks down Oak Street in the morning up Oak Street in the evening, a tall husky man with a slight limp special black leather shoes one sole and heel thicker than the other wears a suit and tie carries a briefcase works in town somewhere every morning asks to use the bathroom spends ten minutes in there stinks up the office something awful. He's polite opens the window closes the door behind him thanks us much relieved though lately my father gives him the key to the ladies' room asks him to go out there. Periodically the Jenney Company sends inspectors around to check on service in stations the inspectors gas up use the bathrooms note how friendly service is and the overall cleanliness of the station. My father's won several little plaques for clean rest rooms he hangs on their walls. One night someone breaks in through the men's bathroom window steals some cash and tools my father believes it's someone who knows the station where the money and tools are maybe the Valiant brothers who live behind the station next to Joe and Red they're the only ones capable of such a thing Joe says they steal cars and shoplift. A friend of my father's has this beautiful one-year-old German shepherd he can't keep so we take her as a watchdog, her real name's Countess my father calls her Condess so we call her Condess until one day my father's friend comes in and when he sees her he calls her Countess Countess I ask yes Countess. We have bathroom windows barred and since we've had Countess around there haven't been any more break-ins though one night my father's getting ready to close a guy walks in out of nowhere holds my father up at pistol point makes off with several hundred dollars cash while Countess is asleep out back.

I'M WEARING KNEE-HIGH rubber boots standing in smelly black sludge dropped Mrs. Amerault's keys down the grate in the garage floor, if I move abruptly sludge slips down into my boots bend over work muck with my hands feeling for keys. More muck I turn over worse the smell can't find the keys but several wrenches screwdrivers and pliers fallen through the grate over the years. An hour in the abyss can't take the smell any longer Blackie pulls me out my father's angry calls Mrs. Amerault she's upset because her house keys are on the chain my father assures her they're lost in the drainage grate no one will find them. He drives to her house in Melrose for her spare set when they're both back at the station shows her the drainage grate you don't have to worry no one will find them down there but she's not pleased. Mrs. Amerault's a serious woman doesn't smile much she's got short, wire-curly gray-blue hair, a grayish complexion and sharp blue eyes. She's a schoolteacher lives with another woman who's a schoolteacher Blackie says they're not the kind of women who like men — when she leaves my father lectures me my mind's always someplace else when will I learn to pay attention. Blackie calls me Floyd the second it's the kind of thing Floyd would do my stomach's unsettled from the sickly smell sludge turning over my hands and feet stained black scrub them with a scrub brush days before they're back to normal. People get angry when gas prices rise two cents per gallon they complain to my father who explains prices are dictated from the Jenney Company and everyone else's gas prices have gone up but they believe he's trying to pull a fast one on them go down the street Freddy's Sunoco he says up three cents a gallon there. Hard to keep the station warm in winter soon as the garage door's open heat gets sucked outside leave the garage door open a second too long he yells close the door what do you think I'm heating Oak Street. When a car's running inside the garage during winter we attach a rubber exhaust hose to the tailpipe and run it out a hole in the garage door from outside exhaust fumes pour out colder the temperatures denser the exhaust fumes. My father records how much gas pumped how much remains in main tanks and once a week we check the level with a long wooden pole with inches marked off, drop the pole down into the tanks measure the depth x

amount of inches on the pole equals x amount
gallons in the tanks. Most customers order gas
in dollars' worth or a fill but old timers tend to
order in gallons, usually five or ten like the old
days. By the way he walks into the garage asks if
they can get their car inspected I know something's
different about him. He's thin with red unkempt
hair and beard wears short shorts and a pair of
rubber thongs emphasizes the s's when he says
can we get an inspection ssticker Blackie and my
father look at each other smile bring the car in
the guy walks out yells Lawrence, Lawrence, the
man says to bring the car in. Lawrence drives the
Volvo in Blackie guides him he's a quiet man can't
tell if he pronounces his s's way the other guy does,
he stands and watches proceedings seemingly
amused and skeptical at the same time. The first
guy's friendly asks Blackie questions what are you
checking when you lift the car up ball joints and
tie-rod ends. I've heard about queers and once
at Jimmy's Cleaners I saw a magazine called *Hot
Rods* men doing all sorts of things together after
looking at it awhile I got an erection like seeing
women do things with each other arouses I wonder do these two guys like photos of women with

women or men with women some folks like it all
Blackie says people who like it both ways are
bisexual Tommy says Doris Day is bisexual I don't
believe it. Their car passes inspection I lick the
inspection sticker place it on the windshield
Blackie says to the first guy okay Sunshine that'll
be a buck the guy pays, backs out, once they leave
the lot my father walks around the garage on
his tiptoes mocks the red haired guy says oh
Lawrence, oh Lawrence. I tell Tommy and George
about the guys Tommy says in the service they
had one of those fruits in their squad he and the
other guys hid parts of his uniform and locked
him outside at night in his underwear until finally
the guy got discharged everyone knew something
was up with that fruit he never wanted to go pussy
hunting with the rest of the guys. George says
more of those types around the more pussy there
is for guys like us.

THE PHONE RINGS middle of the night it's a tow call
he asks the usual questions — is the car locked
or unlocked, is it north or south of Roosevelt

Circle, is there a police cruiser at the scene? During school vacations he wakes me to go with him he's bought a second tow truck though there's barely enough business for the first he's taken out a loan for the new one which is four years old. It's a long boxy truck with a big cab and an oversized boom on the back, bigger than the old truck capable of towing tractor trailers though we don't tow tractor trailers my father says there are many truck companies in the area he can pick up extra jobs the truck will pay for itself and more. Tom Riordan's secretary writes a business letter Oak Street Jenney has a new tow truck capable of towing up to x amount of tons available twenty-four hours a day mail them out to all the truck companies in the area weeks anxiously await but not one response. Blackie says truck companies have their own tow trucks told my father before my father bought the new truck but my father bought it anyhow Tom Riordan secured a second towing plate and towing plates are hard to come by only so many allotted cost thousands of dollars you have to know someone in order to obtain one. Tom tells my father take advantage of having another towing plate if business doesn't work out sell the truck and the plate which he can turn a profit on. Several months the large blue wrecker sits outside unused until my father puts the truck up for sale several months later someone from one of the truck companies makes an offer my father refuses. Another month passes no takers my father calls the man at the truck company back this time the guy offers him less than the first offer my father grudgingly accepts then sells the towing plate for several thousand dollars but he's lost money having the truck around all these months. If it's a school night he goes on tow calls alone an hour or so later returns he's not a good sleeper spends the night on the living room sofa smoking until it's time to open the station then throughout the day he's tired and irritable sleeps through the afternoon in the tow truck or on a bed of tires in the garage where's your father people ask gassing up sleeping I tell them he didn't get much sleep last night. Christmas dinner just finished the antipasto my mother's about to drop raviolis into boiling water phone rings State Police need a tow truck on the Route 28 overpass where it crosses over Interstate 93. My father says he doesn't tow Route 28 but they need him anyway there's another tow truck on the scene a black 1964 Oldsmobile 98's seesawing precariously over the guardrail it'll take two trucks to get it off. The Olds teeters back and forth over the guard rail rocking like it might slide off and fall straight down onto busy Interstate 93 below. The police block lanes off on 93 direct traffic around in case but there's a line of cars parked in the breakdown lane their occupants stand outside watching the proceedings. Each time the wind picks up the Olds begins to rock people start wows and ahhs and my father says it's fucking Christmas don't they have anything else to do state trooper says people love a catastrophe. My father and Phil from Phil's Tow debate the safest way to get the black Olds off the guardrail, if they lift it the wrong way the weight shifts it goes over the side and cables on the truck winches won't hold it. The Oldsmobile's driver is a priest came around the turn too fast spun out flipped over and landed up on the guard-rail. He's an elderly man with a bad toupee who gets out of the cruiser so drunk he can barely walk the trooper rushes over I thought I told you to stay in the cruiser the priest points to the car tries to talk but too drunk the trooper takes him by the arm and leads him back to the cruiser. My father and Phil agree to hook the Oldsmobile on each of its sides, line the trucks up at a certain angle and simultaneously pull. They hook their cables and we wait for more police cruisers to arrive so they can close off a small stretch of Route 28 before and after the bridge and close off a bigger stretch of Route 93 below. Finally several local police cruisers from Medford and Stoneham clear away observers from the breakdown lane, close the other stretches of road, my father and Phil signal each other go and the black Oldsmobile comes flying off of the guardrail smash lands on four wheels in the middle of Route 28. The priest gets out of the cruiser again staggers towards the Olds as if he's going to get in and drive away but the trooper walks him back to the cruiser. All four of the tires on the Olds are flat so my father lifts up its rear end with his truck and Phil slides the dolly under the rear wheels so he can tow it from the front. Back home I'm biting into the raviolis I recount the story black Oldsmobile seesawing back and forth over the main highway phone rings State Police barracks brought the priest to his parish going to try to keep the incident quiet, Phil agrees not to charge the priest for the tow my father says if it's okay with Phil it's okay with me. The priest has a record driving drunk the church anxious not to have the accident go public anyone else would be in jail right now my father says biting into his raviolis.

A. J. TERANI TRADES in his Cadillac every two years his second wife's much younger than he though he talks about his grandchildren from his first wife. He likes two-door coupes currently a 1965 red Eldorado convertible with a white top owns a construction company his charge card reads A. J. Terani Construction Joe says that he's a mob man. Mr. Terani's the most impeccably groomed man I know thick wavy silver hair neatly cut and combed wears expensive sport coats and suits my father says those Italian shoes can't be found under a hundred dollars a pair. Twelve months a year he sports a tan his skin's tough and leathery his second wife's always tanned too her skin I taste in dreams. He wears several big rings and a gold watch manicures his nails notice when he signs his charge slip — clean, shiny, trimmed. A. J. Terani never actually signs his name but two swirling loops which are supposed to be his initials A.J. His young wife has long red hair sometimes teased up wears short skirts long lovely legs her cleavage take my time washing the windshield steal quick glimpses she usually wears sunglasses not sure she's noticing me noticing her. Once or twice a year he has the oil changed on his Cadillac people who trade cars in every two years do little regular maintenance won't own vehicles long enough for regular maintenance to pay off. A. J. Terani's an associate of Tom Riordan my father says he's well connected whenever we're on the highway and there's construction going on most trucks bulldozers and steamrollers have the name A. J. Terani Construction painted on the doors. How many trucks does Mr. Terani own I ask he's got more trucks and money than he'll ever know what to do with. Phil says that A. J. Terani's second wife was a stripper he remembers seeing her strip years ago at a club downtown this was before he went into the service but how can you forget a body like that.

WATER TROUGH LIKE in western movies during fights men get punched into horses drink from we use mostly washing our hands reach into tin can of gelatinous mechanic's soap cool squish scoop lather hands and bottom of arms remove grease from most recent job rinse off in trough three quarters full. The old man only allows us to dump and refill it two or three times a day after several washings the water's sickly gray hot days when he's not around we refill it often Blackie and I stick our heads in cool off. Lenny holds my head down in the water until I'm panicking swallowing water breathing it up my nose. Working under cars held up by a floor jack use the jack stands my father warns fuck the jack stands Lenny says. I use the trough look for tire leaks overinflate the tire submerge it in the trough, turn slowly keep close eye out for that first trace of bubbles indicates location of a puncture. Tires with tubes make more work 'cause I've got to break the tire down from the rim on the machine remove the tube fill it with air and check it in the trough and if the leak's repairable rough up the puncture area with sandpaper spread glue torch the glue until it bubbles blow it out then press on a patch. More

and more tires are tubeless repair them with a plug
and glue hard to believe a little rubber plug and
glue can repair a tire puncture so the tire holds a
car's weight though sometimes they don't my father doesn't like these new tubeless tires Billy Lipo
owns Lipo Trucking gasses up here says he'll never
use tubeless tires in his trucks. I don't know why
Billy Lipo calls his company Lipo Trucking it's
really only a dump truck and steamroller they haul
around on a trailer mostly they do driveway hot
top work. Some days never end sit restlessly in
the office watch the clock listen to the radio the
old man's off somewhere Blackie's out back working on his car reread the *Record American* study
the entertainment section ads for the clubs downtown girls girls girls what can it mean no cover
charge.

GAS FUMES WAFT into my nostrils squeeze the nozzle
hear gas rise up the hose swish of it through the
nozzle. Summertime gas through the nozzle's
metal cool in winter warm. Tumblers click dollars and cents gallons and tenths. How many more

gallons will I pump in my lifetime hundreds of thousands of gallons I'll be here awhile. Hon Annie asks will you pull my car around fill it up her Mustang's got a V-8, automatic chrome stick floor shift, leather bucket seats I back it up to the premium pump how does she maneuver around in here when she's with a guy Billy Coniglio at school says they do it in the car not much you can do with bucket seats and shifter between backseat's small and tight. Annie pays me thanks hon leaves Joe says be nice to Annie you never know what might happen. Dollars and gallons tumble to closing time read the multidigit figure under the dollar and gallon digits on each pump, subtract that number from previous day's clos-ing figure determine exactly how many gallons-to-the-tenth pumped on that pump that day — multiply that figure times the amount per gallon to find how much should be in the gas cash roll minus the twenty dollars started out with at the beginning of the day. We don't ring each gas sale up whoever works the pumps carries a cash roll with him, usually it balances within fifty cents at the end of the day sometimes when Tommy works we're short a ten or twenty. My hands constantly reek gasoline skin's perpetually dried, cracked, dirty white. I've a nozzle on automatic for a fill kicks back gas splashes my eyes on fire multiple washings of cool water. If my father tows a car and no one claims it after sixty days my father legally inherits the vehicle. Joe gets the most destitute car spit-shined inside and out showroom new. My father does whatever work's needed to get the car running, repairs any small dents scratches and trimming, puts it out front on the lot with a for sale sign. It sells. If he's got floating cash my father'll buy a used car when he comes across a good deal and with little work except for a good cleaning he turns a good buck selling it. This 1956 Ford Customline Victoria, black with red interior sharpest car he's ever had, he likes it too been driving it around with his repair plate shiny and ready for a for sale sign for two weeks but hasn't put the sign on it yet. Can we keep it no it's a two-door we need a four-door for a family car but he'll get stuck on the car and keep it today after school it's gone and for a good price. Freddy Golar drives straight into our fence with his 1962 Ford Falcon Christ he says stumbling out the passenger door I didn't think I was that close. Not much damage to the chain-link fence but the left side of his front quarter panel's scratched. Sonny he says hands me the keys will ya move it for me and I do. He's on about something I'm telling ya it's a disgrace yelling into my father's ear Freddy not today I'm not in the mood. He's not in the mood he says to me, Sonny I seen two world wars served in one of 'em and he's not in the mood. Freddy leave the kid alone he's got work to do go out and help Blackie with that exhaust system if you've nothing to do. I can hear them in the office the old man yells Freddy leave me the fuck alone a few moments later Freddy's out pestering us, boys I've been through two world wars and Blackie's about to light the acetylene torch so he can cut through an old exhaust system Freddy if you don't want your ass singed you better be out of my way too. Freddy grumbles then back in the office shouts I don't have to take this shit at my father and leaves. It takes him five minutes to get his car started and drive off the lot with all his starts and stops. Blackie puts his goggles on hands me a pair I put them on hold up the end of an exhaust system he's cutting through. Blackie's careful wearing goggles and taking precautions Lenny never does I get a tiny chip rusty exhaust metal in my eye like stuck with a pin try washing it out my father takes me to the hospital the doctor drops different colored liquids in my eye removes the metal chip washes my eye out over and over wear a patch rest of the day tiny painful wound pesters for days always wear goggles working on exhaust systems goggled Blackie says freshly lit Pall Mall hangs out his mouth torch in his hand working the rusty metal exhaust pipe shades of blue and blaze orange the torch cuts through muffler and tailpipe fall into my arms.

HIDE MY CIGARETTES in Blackie's toolbox he smokes filterless Pall Malls I prefer Marlboros but buy Pall Malls so my father doesn't get suspicious seeing Marlboros in Blackie's toolbox. Joe and Red smoke Camels my favorite filterless, during summer Red rolls a fresh pack upper sleeve of his white T-shirt, stands arms folded in blue jeans, pointed boots, greased back red hair, on-deck Camel placed behind his right ear like he's carved from marble. Girls have always loved Red Joe says Red's got a big monster a sight to behold with all that red hair brother James who burned to death in the tunnel fire was the shy one but Red's never had any problem with the ladies. Red helps Joe with cleanings and polishings most of the time Red just hangs out, the house they live in is paid for all they must do is take care of the upkeep and their mother. Red removes a half pint from his right rear pocket breaks the seal unscrews the cap and in three attempts empties its contents. That stuff will kill him says Joe who can't drink hard stuff an ulcer but finishes a case of beer in a half day and Joe probably all of 120 pounds. There's an old friend of George's just moved up from the south living in a little automobile trailer the old man lets him park behind the station for a week. He's a scary looking guy — short, dark, blackhead-embedded facial skin, dirty greased back black hair, sunken mouth from false teeth and in the middle of conversation he'll pop his upper choppers out and make an ugly face. Calls me stupid little guinea prick but gives me cigarettes whenever I ask says he'll buy beer for me appear at his trailer now parked behind a

junkyard on Riverside Ave. he's got a six-pack of
Private Stock malt liquor. I'm smashed halfway
through my second he starts getting close to me,
grabs my dick push his hand away stop what's
wrong don't you like sex yeah but not with men.
Have you ever done it with a man no have you
ever done it with a woman no then how do I know
whether I like men or women. He's got a point
but if I did want to do it with a man it certainly
wouldn't be him he rubs my dick again push him
away backs me into a corner of the tiny trailer's
kitchenette pushes his body against mine moves
to kiss me I turn my head away and with all my
strength manage to sidestep him knocking over
my half-filled beer at the same time. I'll be real
gentle he says I'll like it moves towards me again
better get the fuck out of here grab my jacket he
grabs my shoulder don't go I'll stop I head for
the trailer door he says keep this between us we
don't want my father to find out I've been drinking. I'm afraid to tell anyone wonder if George
knows about his friend for weeks the image of
that wild-eyed foul-breathed creep coming after
me.

SEWELL D. FRANK SPEAKS in soft mumbles I say pardon me and what after he says something. He's a dull quirky man an engineer at MIT I'm not sure what MIT is but Tommy says it's a college for people who are smart but don't have a lick of common sense. Blackie says Mr. Frank's one of those geniuses whose head's in the clouds, incapable of everyday kind of thinking. Mr. Frank's odd looking, medium build, midforties, bald, wears glasses, pale complexion, thin lips and flat nose, twice a week purchases ten gallons of gas and has me check *everything* under the hood including his oil, transmission fluid, brake fluid, radiator water, battery water, belts and hoses. I don't understand why he needs to check all of this stuff it's only been three days since he was last here stands guard over me as I dip the dipstick, show him on the stick full to the line, same with the transmission fluid and when I pop the top of the master cylinder he looks in to see the brake fluid's full then the radiator and battery and if one of the battery cylinders is down a fraction of an inch of water he has me top it off then watches me check belts and hoses for tightness. A radiator hose should be solid rubber to the touch too dry it should be replaced before it cracks and leaks. I complain to Blackie why does Mr. Frank make me check all that stuff every time there's no way a hose or a radiator can go bad that quickly and if the oil's right up there one day it'll surely be up there three days later if Mr. Frank has only driven a hundred miles. Mr. Frank's one of those peculiar people he says engineers tend to be like that spend their lives studying all that cause and effect stuff in the rain I go around with a tire gauge check the tire pressure never once has one of his tires been below 28 pounds. Servicing Mr. Frank's 1961 De Soto with the two-tiered grille and shark-nose taillights he shadows me in the garage watching every move with his car up on the lift making certain I don't miss any grease fittings or that I put enough grease in all of them. Can you put a little more grease in that lower left ball joint I squeeze the grease gun hard grease comes shooting out from the fitting I nail him with a glob of grease sorry he backs away takes a rag wipes the top of his bald head but it doesn't stop him moments later he's right next to me breathing down my neck. Sewell D. Frank what kind of name is Sewell D. Frank I ask my father and

Blackie says it's a pretty fucking stupid name my father says it's Jewish.

No sooner my hair falls over my ears he hands me a buck go to Jimmy's cut your hair. Jimmy's barbershop is two blocks up and down a side street his shop's located on the first floor of a three-story tenement. Jimmy's open two afternoons and Saturdays he's got a full-time job cutting hair at a hospital on the other days two guys ahead of me good to kill some time get a break new *Playboy* calendar up in the bathroom and girlie magazines top of the toilet tank I don't have to go to the bathroom enough time to check out all twelve months on the calendar July 1967 my favorite. My father's cousin Lucy lives upstairs from Jimmy's in one of the apartments sees me going into the barbershop come up when you're through for a sandwich or dish of macaroni. Lucy and her husband Al always in the kitchen on the phone rings all day they're writing figures and initials on their notepaper, names of horses in the fourth, how to play today's trifecta, who's up

who's down. Not sure Lucy's really my father's
cousin Lucy's family and my father's family are
commadre, somewhere between family and close
friend. My father's on the phone with Lucy and
Al at least once a day and often hangs out up there
drinking coffee and smoking cigarettes it's a small
apartment, cramped rooms, low ceilings, during
summer dreadfully hot few windows poor ventilation hum-click of kitchen window fan does little
to alleviate. Hottest days cars overheat several
times per day drivers clank onto the station lot
steam shooting out from under the hood never
touch the radiator cap until the engine's off and
the cooling system has a chance to cool down or
it can blow and spray scalding hot water my
father's right arm scarred from a radiator cap that
blew just below his tattoo in Italian reads MOTHER
YOU SUFFER FOR ME. First snow means snow tire
sales and service, rainy days mean electrical problems, cold weather brings dead batteries, hot days
spew faulty cooling systems I'm sure of these
things season to season.

PARTS STORE'S STUFFY smell rubber, metals, petroleum products and assorted chemicals. Long busy counters lined with thousand-page books listing hundreds of thousands of parts, parts men with phones pressed between their ears and shoulders flip through myriad grime-bemarked pages with dirty fingers, numbers, years, makes and models narrow down one particular part and its corresponding part number. Phone conversations of makes and models, Starfire or 88, was a 'sixty-two you said, two-door or four-door, V-6 or V-8, automatic or standard transmission, I don't see it listed let me check another book. There's good money to be made in parts, my father charges list, buys at a considerable discount and won't install parts purchased elsewhere — you don't bring your own food into a restaurant. The woman who works in the sub shop next to the parts store looks a little like my mother olive skin small frame straight dark brown hair she keeps in a ponytail large brown eyes protruding nose I think she and my father have a thing for each other. Yesterday he sold the '62 Volkswagen Beetle's been sitting out front five months for sale, someone walks in off the street how much my father says $400 without making a counteroffer the man says he'll take it and returns in an hour with cash. My father picks up the car for nothing it needs a clutch which costs $40. He's gone all day today I'm sure he's at the track that cash burning a hole in his pocket. In the morning when we open up someone has to scoop last night's piles of Countess's shit strewn all over the garage floor. Using the little broom and shovel from one pile to the next don't know how one dog can shit so much doesn't matter when we feed her morning noon or evening she shits around the clock and turd duty's tough first thing in the morning my breakfast is waiting in the office I love the radio but my father wants to listen to WBZ for local news and traffic in the morning, later in the day he's off somewhere I listen to WRKO Beatles Stones Who. Blackie likes the oldies station plays music from the fifties Chuck Berry and Little Richard Blackie says that was rock and roll not that noisy crap I listen to can't understand the words what does he make of Little Richard womp bomp baluma awomp bam boom? My father likes sports baseball basketball hockey baseball's his first choice nothing so boring as listening to a baseball game on the radio. He listens to radio talk shows at night tunes into "Sports Talk" followed by Larry Glick I can't believe how stupid some of the callers who mumble and when Larry asks what's your point they don't have an answer must call just to hear themselves talk. He looks up at the clock and starts fidgeting. I wait on a gas customer he makes a phone call ends abruptly as I enter the office then within a few minutes hands me the gas cash roll he's got to go see someone about a used car disappears until closing time. I switch to WRKO, smoke, drink cold Pepsis, new girlie magazine in the desk drawer. During the summer bathe Countess every week she gets filthy around the station, she loves her baths stretches her back out her head raised in the air brush out all her excess hair, hose her down, lather her up, rinse her off, then do it all again when I'm finished she runs off and rolls around in some grime. I take her up to the pond and bathe her there after hours they don't want me washing my dog where people swim tonight look at the new girlie magazine George dropped off. When I first looked at nude photographs of women in magazines I believed the images painted or fabricated somehow.

BUSINESS IS SLOW sweep the lot a light breeze blows neat little piles I make. Keep an eye out for stray screws or sharp pieces of metal endlessly coming to rest on the ground always something you can be doing my father says I take my time when I'm through there's a pump island to paint or the back corner of the garage to clean where stuff's piling up from various jobs — old engine heads, tire rims, an intake manifold from a 283 Chevy engine, a radiator, wheel drums, carburetors, all usable with a little work enough potential value saved them from the trash. I notice him eyeballing the pile this morning at the pumps soon as one car pulls in there's a run of others. I put the broom aside seven or eight customers in a row several at once. I handle at least two at a time, the key is the car's positioning so I can use both pumps at once get one fill started wash the windshield quickly get second car started first car's still filling wash the windshield on the second and it goes smoothly until someone wants only a dollar's worth and another wants me to check under the hood but I keep the line moving. You're a young boy to be doing all of this yourself I'll be thirteen. Resume sweeping he's in the office drinking heavy cream penciling the racetrack section of the *Record American* on the phone with Vito soon he'll barrel off to Rockingham in Vito's Caddy. Vito owns part of a racing horse my father's talking buying in with him my mother doesn't like the idea won't stop him if he's determined. I finish sweeping he says got some things to do be back later help Blackie if he needs me or organize the pile out in the far corner of the garage calls Vito be there in a couple of minutes. Light a cigarette switch the radio station Blackie's tuning a '62 Chevy Impala that smooth straight six won't need me except to turn the ignition when he sets the distributor cam high lobe to adjust points and condenser. Then he starts taking apart the engine he's rebuilding from a '61 Volkswagen go down the Jew's and get us some Devil Dogs and milk. Devil Dogs and milk, ice-cold milk, Blackie's favorite things to eat and drink. He takes a buck out of his wallet and I walk down to Harry's buy Devil Dogs and a quart of milk Harry your father doesn't like me but I never did anything to your father warm afternoon light passing through greeny dull storefront window illuminates him hands out to his sides palms open I tell you I just don't understand people.

NEVER WITHOUT A cut or abrasion on one or both of my hands try to loosen a génerator nut wrench slips my knuckle comes down hard on edge of the generator pulley bloody gash my right knuckle wash it bandage it impossible to keep clean though it doesn't get infected Blackie says dirt and grease heal by sealing an open wound that's why mechanics never get infections with all the great cuts and abrasions they receive that swell turn different colors blue and grime black scabs. Rusty exhaust systems are dangerous layers paper-thin sharp old metal can cut right through bone Freddy at Freddy's Sunoco's lost the tip of his middle finger. During winter my hands always cracked gaping open cracks on my knuckles bleed the more I wash my hands the worse they get sometimes use lotion Tommy says only a woman would use lotion on her hands but even with lotion the cracks remain until the weather warms. Blackie's torching through the exhaust manifold pipe on an Olds 98 I'm holding up the back, one hand on the tailpipe one on the muffler, shift my weight let go the muffler one second suddenly the bracket gives way whole exhaust system comes crashing down in the middle of the garage floor Blackie and I run out from under narrowly missing blows to the head Jesus Fucking Christ Blackie says reaching down for the torch fallen on the floor still blowing fire shuts it off. My father and I are out on road service four degrees above zero he cuts his hand on the under edge of a car's hood hardly notices until back into the tow truck after jump-starting the car in the heat of the cab blood fountains forth from my father's left palm gashed open and deep cold froze the blood and it didn't thaw until the heat of the cab the emergency room they stitch him up. I rub lotion into tender sore open knuckle cracks they burn and bleed until spring.

SQUIRRELS AND BIRDS live in the small stand of trees back of the station where a little hill rises to backyards of Gaston Street houses. Let Countess off the chain she runs around sniffing out discarded tires oil cans a shopping carriage rusting on its side. She never shits where I want her to no matter when I feed her she shits right around her house where we keep her chained and in the garage and office at night. Light a smoke, walk into the thick foliage unseen, sit down on the overturned carriage. Countess sniffs around takes short pisses on different things Mrs. Terani gassed up this morning her blue Thunderbird convertible miniskirt bathing suit top, tanned, freckled, long thick red hair bound by a bandanna rest blows behind her when she drives her breasts concealed so slightly beneath her black swimsuit top don't care if she is watching me watch her from behind her sunglasses work the squeegee back and forth. I rub it she rushes up jumps on me my father's calling. Blackie says Mrs. Terani has a pool in her backyard once he went to start her car she was sunbathing by the pool in a bikini looking like a goddess oil gleaming in the sun. I chain Countess she immediately shits next to her house where the hell were you out back letting the dog run around. Someone's driven in with a flat tire and he wants me to fix it. In the old days he says he worked hard but my father's adept at doing as little as possible, the only thing he gets enthused about is a tow call. He lives for the telephone to ring with a call from the State Police then gets all excited barking out orders get Mr.

Lampry's wagon in for a grease and oil while I'm gone runs full tilt to the tow truck like an ambulance driver tears out of the lot orange and red lights flashing and turning drives wildly beeping the horn for people to get out of his way yelling don't you see these lights as if he's going to a life or death struggle when often a car's out of gas or a flat tire. I jack up the car and remove the left front tire fill it with air and place it in the water trough bubbles up through water tire's picked up what looks to be a roofing nail I remove plug the tire and place it back on the car. There's something nauseating about the smell of air blown through rubber whether I'm pumping air into a tire or letting air out. I plunge my hands into the can of gelatinous goo of mechanic's soap Mrs. Terani leave them submerged squeezing goo between my fingers.

HE'S SEEING THE woman who works in the sub shop next to the parts store where he's been hanging out drinking coffee and smoking fine with Blackie and me because he's out of our way at the station. We get our morning coffee and donuts at Town Line Donuts but he changes to the shop next door to the parts store ten minutes out of the way donuts taste old I now know for sure the way his mood elevates when he's in there making little jokes teasing she yawns what are you yawning for didn't you sleep last night all the while his wide smile not enough not enough she answers. When my mother catches him with my fifth-grade schoolmate's mother she throws him out for two months and he lives in a rooming house in Malden. I see him nearly every day he picks me up after school or at home on Saturday mornings asks how's your mother doing complains how unhappy he is the woman who owns the rooming house is so cheap he pleads with her turn up the heat. Back at home kisses my mother before going to work in the morning and when he arrives home at night, this goes on for a few months. He goes bankrupt the first time he runs the gas station during the 1950s he's only in America three years when he takes over the business in 1952. I'm only around for an afternoon once a week elementary school a big thing just to pump gas he gambles every penny away she catches him trying to cash in savings bonds put away for me and my sister he owes a lot of money the phone's ringing men are looking for him hangs up the phone unnerved. He files for bankruptcy my mother can't take the gambling he's got to move out and does for a month takes me and my sister for rides and ice cream cries he wants to come home we cry and back home plead with her take him back she does. Several years later the Jenney Company contacts him again two recent proprietors failed to make the station go if he's interested they'll help him get the station back. He's driving cab and on Saturdays takes me with him with a little kid in the front seat he gets better tips talk with businessmen in suits with briefcases on their way to the airport for places like Atlanta and San Francisco and Germany they tip my father and sometimes me too. He's not earning enough driving cab, days are long, too long for one who's already had a taste of having others work for him so he takes the station again — they kick off with a huge grand opening complete with my father's usual special event fanfare mechanical man out front, flags, clowns, free glassware with a fill-up, balloons for kids and all his old customers turn out. Why does he choose women who look like my mother this new one's younger than my mother divorced has a daughter he's always particular about how much heat and electricity we waste. During the winter he's constantly on me about keeping the garage door openings and closings to a minimum, at night he puts lights on one at a time, first he switches on the Jenney sign which is illuminated from within, some kind of red, white and blue plastic exterior with the word J E N N E Y in red. The old sign was made of wood, letters hand painted, lit from lights on the outside. Years of pestering the Jenney Company and taking Bill Gleason home for dinner lead to the new sign. Ours is the last station in the city with an old wooden sign and old-fashioned narrow gas pumps. Along with the Jenney sign pump lights light up directly behind the glass on the pump so you can see the tumblers and know the amount. The new pumps have the tumbler light and a light that illuminates the regular and premium letters on top of the pump, and above the pump island are two big fluorescent lamps which light the pump island area and much of the station yard. As soon as it's dark first of these lights goes on. They take several minutes to warm up and reach maximum potential. He never turns the second island light on but if he's not going to be around I turn them both on brightens up the yard makes the place look like it's got some life. The office light's on when it's dark and the garage is kept dark whenever it's not in use. I get my father's old uniforms when he and the mechanics switch over to new every year so I wear short baggy pants squeezed tight around the waistline by a belt and an oversized faded blue shirt with my father's name on it. During summer I wear a T-shirt and jeans though he insists I wear the full uniform T-shirt and jeans look sloppy. All afternoon my mouth waters thoughts of pepper and egg sandwiches my mother has promised for supper. Now that I'm eating I'm put off too much olive oil's seeped through thick crusty pieces of bread, the paper wrap, and lunch bag she brought it in. Halfway through the first sandwich feel slightly nauseous out back of the garage where Countess is sleeping give the sandwiches to her she chomps them up and swallows with aggressive methodical mouth and throat movements. Nausea passes I'm hungry and the old man's off for the night nothing to eat I'm hoping that one of the guys will come around get me a sub. My mother's idea of dessert is fruit and the pear she put in the bag got soaked by the olive oil from the pepper and egg sandwiches. The phone rings a woman's voice from the sub shop when do I expect him back closing time. I thought he was with her must be at the dog track saw him with Wonderland schedule this afternoon. I smoke three cigarettes in a row and my nausea returns in the bathroom I'm going to throw up but only dry heave.

MOST PAY CASH a few use credit cards means I have to go into the office run the card through fill out the slip bring it back to the customer to sign with their copy and bring the merchant copy back into the office. At the end of the week list every credit transaction by hand on a Jenney Company form which I forward to the Jenney Company. Jenney's a small company there aren't any Jenney stations outside New England rumor is they'll merge with a bigger company. We give credit to some long-standing regular customers and friends who pay by the month or sometimes not records are kept in a small metal file box slips for private accounts many long overdue folks for one reason or another never return to pay their bills. Danny Walsh and my father play cards together still lives a few blocks away hasn't been in for over a year he and his wife have lots of kids little money drink heavily Danny doesn't keep jobs. He's into my father for six months of gas and repairs on his beat up old Pontiac wagon held together by wire and string Blackie says. Danny stops attending card games and coming to the station, we see him around town he looks the other way why not ask him for the money my father says Danny wouldn't have it. We haven't seen Lou Gioisa the bread man for two years. Lou delivers bread for one of the South Medford bakeries, working on his truck's tough too big too high to use the lift use a jack I change the oil on my back on a creeper grease the fittings with an old-fashioned hand-pump grease gun. Lou's in over his head with the bookies owes people all over the city in South Medford Jimmy's Cleaners has a sign in the window reads LOU OWES ME TOO. One thing I never see is a bottom line. Don't know how much he brings in for sure but during inspection time Blackie's flat out, Joe, Floyd, Tiny, Me and Tommy at different times flat out too. The money for the inspection sticker is clear profit sometimes we inspect hundreds of cars a week and all the revenue from extra repair work adds up. There are weeks he makes a thousand dollars but he overspends at the track or card games, buys a new tow truck, gives Johnny Calderone six hundred bucks a year and a half ago doesn't hear from him since. Johnny's an old biker friend of Blackie's hangs around the station doesn't have a job but rides an impeccable full-dressed Harley lives with his girlfriend Denise every time I see her I beat off for days her blond teased-up hair and tight black jeans high-heeled shoes black fishnet stockings skimpy summertime tops get hard watching her wrap her hair up in a kerchief, put her motorcycle helmet on and climb up onto the back of that full dresser sitting legs apart, high heels on the footrests, slender white arms wrapped around Johnny's big belly. Johnny's a short powerful guy shaved head big gold earring tattooed arms like tree trunks. Johnny's got a friend who's a horse trainer in the know about races at Suffolk and Rockingham gives Johnny tips Johnny and my father end up with several impressive winnings at the track one day he's got a tip borrows three hundred from my father my father puts up three hundred of his own Johnny's off to Suffolk and that's the last time anyone's heard from Johnny. Word is he ripped off several others same way same day Blackie thinks he left the state says Johnny would steal from his own mother. I don't get paid for my time at the station but when I'm sixteen I can have a car and he'll take care of the expenses. My first car's an old Ford a '49 stripped and engineless parked for several months in the back of the station I'm ten years old spend hours behind the steering wheel driving listen to the radio make up my own songs stop for gas my father laughs says I gas up a lot. One day the car's sent off to the junkyard he says there'll be another second's a '59 Volkswagen needs an engine and a paint job Blackie and I rebuild the engine Blackie gives it a bad paint job fire engine red I drive it around the station lot for two weeks then my father sells it for $250 says we'll find another one before I get my license. It's best when people pay cash paperwork's easier more people pay cash the more money my father can keep off the books. The bookkeeper is a man who looks like Bob Hope his nose is pickled red from drink he has a high-pitched nasally voice, wears striped sport coats and bright bow ties, you're doing all right he assures my father you're doing all right.

How MUCH DOES he spend at the track or on his women gives my mother $75 per week to run the house she's been telling him she needs more he ups it to a hundred. He says he's going to play cards with Tom Riordan who picks him up but Tom doesn't play cards he's got a summer house on a little lake in Marlborough an hour away I think they go there with women. Not one of my father's women but Tom's women there are two a black one and white one Tommy says they're Tom Riordan's regulars and the black one's really something tits out to here he illustrates with his hands. Tom Riordan's married to a beautiful blond woman who has a well-paying state job but rarely goes to work some kind of secretarial thing.

Joe and Tommy say that his wife's had a boyfriend for years she and Tom have an understanding when Tom was running for political office it wouldn't have been okay if he was divorced the marriage became a sort of business arrangement. Tom's not a state representative any longer but he's worth considerable money one of the grandest homes in Medford new cars summer house in Marlborough winter home in Florida and last winter my father went to Florida with Tom for a week's vacation took the two women with them my father worships Tom Tom always picks up the bills costs my father little my mother trusts Tom that's why she didn't say much about my father going to Florida with him he told her he was going to help Tom paint the Florida house. Tom's switched on like he never stopped being a politician perpetual smile scrubbed clean round face hair cut once a week nice blazers ties and well-shined shoes comes to the house the night they are leaving picks up my father and his baggage don't worry I'll keep an eye on him assures my mother. My mother finds out about the woman in the sub shop drives up to the woman's house walks through the front door my father sitting at the kitchen table claims he's there to collect for plowing she puts him out calls a lawyer the lawyer tells her she's got grounds for divorce my father's got a small cot for a week sleeps in the back of the garage picks me up for work at the house asks how's your mother is she still talking with the lawyer suddenly the lawyer's gone he's back in the house not seeing the woman in the sub shop but tonight he's with Tom and Tom's women.

NEEDLE-DICK-the-Bug-Fucker Tommy calls me any smaller he says I'd have to take it out of my pants with a pair of needle-nose pliers. Compared with other kids in showers during gym class I don't seem to have too much more or less Tommy says you can't tell soft. I've never seen one hard except the guys in magazines huge ones I'll bet you don't even hit five inches hard Tommy says how much you want to bet are you going to show me no but I'll show Joe he says five bucks. I go into the bathroom with the new *Playboy* look at the centerfold spread beautiful brunette lounging poolside nervous half hard start to pump it swells want to bring myself off big as it gets call Joe who comes with the ruler places it alongside my you've got a hunk of meat tells Tommy Tommy refuses to pay George and Joe put the squeeze on Tommy pulls five out of his wallet throws it at me here you little prick remember it's not what you got but how you use it and I'm not talking about using it with your hand. Joe says you ought to be putting that thing to use Red and Freddy Golar drive in in Freddy's black Ford Falcon Freddy's so drunk I don't know how he drove them here in one piece. They've got a pint Freddy's shouting Red's eyes and face blaze Tommy throws them out before they get too comfortable. Tommy no trouble no trouble Red repeats but Freddy's loud yelling at Tommy a lot of nerve you got putting me out I won't have it. Tommy says get the fuck out of here and Freddy and Red stagger back out to the Ford Falcon, take a few swigs from the pint in the front seat, then in slow motion Freddy backs up, turns an about-face and drives away. Tommy says they'll be lucky if they don't kill someone or themselves. At home in bed I stroke myself the woman in the *Playboy* lying on her stomach on a chaise lounge, right leg up in the air toes pointing to heaven, water beads on her smooth ass glistening in the sun well tanned except white inside her bikini lines. When he first opens the station my father works for a year by himself seven days a week twelve hours a day. He's not much of a mechanic more of a wire and tape man Blackie calls him Mick the Mouse Take the Easy Way Out. I'm removing a starter nearly electrocute myself forget to disconnect the battery screwdriver strikes live juice starter wire. Blackie gets frustrated but stays cool my father would have thrown a fit over me removing a starter without first disconnecting the battery Blackie says I buy you books and send you to school and nothing happens. My mind endlessly drifts don't hear everything folks say Blackie removing belts from a '60 Mercury says get me a 3/8-inch open end I walk to the toolbox can't remember I'm thinking about going up to the pond with Countess later in the afternoon swimming my shadow in late afternoon clear water light. Three-eighths-inch open end he says voice raised he sees me pause in front of the box. Lots of times thinking about women I'm afraid I'm masturbating too much when I'm in

confession Father Everheart grills me about touch-
ing myself wants to know do I think about girls
and what is it I think about I tell him simple lies
when he comes in for gas I'm afraid he might rec-
ognize me. My father forever strips nuts and bolts
tightening too much or turning the wrong direction pulls on an oil filter so hard with the filter
wrench it slips and pokes a hole in the radiator.
Blackie keeps him out of the garage as much as
possible says that guy could fuck up a wet dream.

MUSIC'S ELECTRIC WILD rhythms and sounds long-
haired music Blackie and Phil call it can't
understand the words how the hell could you get
laid to it if rock and roll's for anything Phil says
it's for getting laid. My friend Jerry Hastings has
all the latest albums the other day at school we
skipped two classes went to his house and listened
to music Jerry plays electric guitar and he's teach-
ing me. Jimi Hendrix this morning on the radio
Blackie climbs out the trunk of a Rambler he's
doing electrical work in shut that fucking shit off.
Phil says give him "In the Still of the Night" I

strip a bolt tightening down a valve cover gasket
hope it won't leak start the engine it leaks Blackie
finds a self-threading bolt close enough to the
original size bolts it in for me be careful with a
self-threading bolt he says go get us a cigarette
Pall Mall unfiltered so strong straightens me up
an inch when I inhale. Phil fidgets with the radio
Chuck Berry "Maybellene" leave it there Blackie
says can't do any better than Chuck. Why can't
you be true Blackie shouts takes a long drag on
his Pall Mall twists a bit with his ass sticking out.
There's trouble at home his beautiful wife drinks
he gets home from work she's drunk they fight
my father tells him you've got to pour that booze
down the sink in front of her and put your foot
down he does and things are quieter now. I need
to get out and have some fun he says throwing
his cigarette down stomps on it and climbs back
into the little brown Rambler's trunk singing why
can't you be true? I fantasize I'm alone with
Blackie's wife she takes me to bed my first hot
radiator cap blasts off doused with hot water
blisters on my chest. I thought the radiator had
cooled enough when will I learn to pay attention
my father wants to know. Late in the afternoon

beach is already deserted undress down to my blue jeans Countess rushes in makes one of her hard striding circles I swim out to the middle of the pond tread water keep Countess and her dog-paddling claws at a distance. Cool water soothes the blisters on my chest could I masturbate out here no one around hard to keep myself afloat with one hand.

THE POLICE FIND the stolen Chrysler New Yorker parked in the back garage my father's taken to the police station for questioning. Al D'Amato's paying my father to store the cars under arrest part of a stolen car ring tells the police my father has no knowledge cars he's been storing are stolen. Two cars out back nearly a year 1961 Lincoln and a 1962 Chrysler New Yorker three weeks ago Al removes the Lincoln so the police find only a Chrysler. Local papers feature the story on page one it makes page four in the *Record American* several dozen under arrest my father's name is saved from the *Record American*'s story but the *Daily Mercury* mentions that one of the stolen cars was recovered at my father's station. My father's called to be a witness at the trial customers and folks around town are talking all about it stolen cars have been found at several area garages and junkyards the owners of which to a person claim ignorance. Al D'Amato's described by the media as one of their ringleaders testifies on the stand my father had no knowledge that the cars he's been paying him to store are stolen. Manny Cabral owns the big junkyard in Malden where seven cars are found Blackie says Cabral Junk's where cars are stripped for parts then put to the cruncher. Other cars marked for out-of-state sales are repainted in Manny's body shop so Manny is indicted too when it's his turn to testify as a witness my father claims all along that he had no idea the cars were stolen and over past couple of years he's stored several cars for Al and never had a problem. Customers question me they question my father he tells them the story of how he thought he was storing cars for people who were going out of state or the country they accept the story or if they don't believe him they don't let on they don't. Several months pass between the time police find the stolen Chrysler and the beginning of the trial by now it's as if it happened in another life my father's talking to his lawyer and Tom Riordan who've been giving him advice the trial lasts for two weeks the stolen car ring is in the newspapers again seven of the twelve men on trial are convicted. Some customers including Mrs. Amerault have not been in since it was first reported that the stolen Chrysler had been discovered at the station. Three of the seven men convicted end up with jail sentences Al D'Amato receives seven to ten but will probably be out in four. After the trial my father's quiet and lethargic weeks of mooning around orders wrong parts and mixes up the lunch orders I'm not sure where he's been going his racetrack friends call for him so he's not with them.

FLICK OF THE compressor switch first thing in the morning *varoom* kicks in runs about fifteen minutes shuts off until we use the lift or power tools or the grease gun which run off the compressor. Early in the morning the compressor's noises annoying by the end of the day I stop noticing.

It's not that he hits me much anymore though he's still capable of lashing out with a backhander when I least expect it, but it's the way he'll nag on about my mind always being somewhere else how next time I'll crack you over the head. During winter kids skate on the pond after school on Saturdays walk by woolen hats and gloves skates over shoulders my father won't allow me to skate on the pond I wouldn't anyway breaking through ice into the cold depths. Countess tries to go out on the ice slips her legs fly out from under her three girls a few feet from shore watch boys play hockey vying for the boys' attention one of them looks over at me awkward in my blue uniform pants and dirty jacket call Countess and leave. I see her several times now walking up Oak Street on her way to or from the pond tight wet blue bathing suit cut deep into her ass cheeks. The lift has a safety mechanism in case the compressor should suddenly shut down while a car's in the air so the car won't come crashing down. I wash the front windshield the rear window if in the mood or not in a hurry and offer to check under the hood which is checking the oil radiator water battery water then I have them start the engine if the car has an automatic transmission because for reasons I can't understand the engine has to be running to check the automatic transmission fluid. Automatic transmissions are at least twice the size of standard transmissions because a standard transmission is very simple gears just gears which fit one into the other. Automatic transmissions have gears and all sorts of valves and seals myriad intricate inner workings most garages won't even work on automatic transmissions send customers to automatic transmission specialists. My father never worked on automatic transmissions until Blackie though Blackie's not comfortable working on them he does. He has an instinct for finding his way, that's where you separate the R & R men who remove and replace from the real mechanic like Blackie never afraid to take on a job he's never done before first time he rebuilds an automatic transmission follows repair manual gently finding his way says key thing is understanding the nature of what's at hand. No carburetor rear end front end transmission or electrical problem he can't fix. I like it raining when don't have to wash the windshields or offer to check under the hood.

HARDLY A DAY passes someone doesn't wander in jacket over shoulder this one out of breath from the trek up Oak Street from Interstate 93 where he left his fuel-less car parked in the breakdown lane. He doesn't want to leave the five-dollar deposit on the gas can no deposit no gas can my father hears him giving me a hard time charges in from the garage what's the problem he doesn't want to leave the deposit no deposit no gas can. The man grudgingly digs into his wallet removes a five I fill the old round dented red with yellow letters FUEL can. Before the deposit policy several folks return to their cars on the highway and just take off now they must return for the deposit fill up at the same time stupidest thing anyone can do is run out of gas my father says. The State Police stop traffic middle lane of the interstate rows of flares cruiser lights whirling car's out of gas I'm pouring two gallons from the can *air-ear-whack* of cars and trucks speeding by in the other lanes my father shouts hurry up from where he's bullshitting with one of the troopers. Blackie's doing an engine job pile of parts for me to scrape and clean spend the afternoon in between gas customers listen to the radio stand over cleaning sink in the garage scraping stuck gasket bits and wire-brushing grime-ridden parts make sure you get all the carbon off the top of those pistons Blackie says. I know all the parts, I know where they go, but I can never reassemble and make it all run.

SATURDAY NIGHT MY fourteenth birthday Joe buys me a six-pack pours me a cold one into a Styrofoam cup hands it to me happy fourteenth little man. I guzzle the contents in a few swallows slow down he says you've got all night it's going to be longer than you think Tommy adds I ask what's up Joe smiles tonight young one you be-come a man. Annie's agreed to breaking me in it's the guys' birthday gift to me I'll be first among all my friends Annie's not my first choice but I can't tell them that Tommy'll say something like beggars shouldn't be choosers and he's right. I press for details when how Joe says be patient and when she arrives later he'll give me a signal I'm to go out back in the big tow truck she'll come along later don't worry trust my instincts Tommy

says tonight you're going to get reamed steamed
and dry-cleaned. What time is she coming will I
need a rubber a hundred-per-minute scenarios
what might happen in the truck alone with Annie.
What should I say to her Tommy says I'm not out
there for a fucking debate I'm out there to fuck
Joe says everything will be fine Annie knows what
she's doing Tommy says better your dick than
mine. Annie arrives says hello walks over gives
me a quick kiss on the lips happy birthday she
says and looks prettier than I remember sweet
taste of her lipstick really not as fat as I thought
Joe offers her a beer she accepts we stand awkward small talk car rolls in over the bell hose
ding-ding Tommy says for me to go out and take
it I tell him he's the one getting paid tonight it's
my birthday calls me ungrateful little prick on his
way out. More small talk I get the signal grab my
cup of beer walk out back there's been much rain
past few days the petroleum-muck puddle is high
lay some boards down over it and as I traverse
them they sink into the mush cause a thick
squisshh sound. It's humid and the smell is rank
between the muck puddle and Countess's shit-
piles so I close the windows in the tow truck sip

my beer in fear that I'm not going to be able to get it up or she gets pregnant. Tommy's given me a rubber with instructions on how to use it afraid I'll go soft when trying to put it on. In a few minutes she walks around the building maneuvering the planks squish into the muck puddle opens the door slide over honey with a smile. Sit in silence a few seconds like an hour don't be nervous everything's going to be fine leans over kisses me softly on the lips her tongue pushes deep into my mouth I give my tongue back don't know when to stop pulls hers back I assume that's enough. Then she leans over and kisses me with her tongue again and I reach up inside her top for her breasts full round softer than imagined underneath her breasts her belly rests over her jeans because of the way she's sitting. I start to rub her breasts slowly I read in men's magazines how a woman likes to be seduced slowly have her breasts fondled her cunt gently licked and how to control oneself not cum too quickly. Her nipples are large and hard like tollhouse cookies can hear Joe say squeeze one between my fingers ooch she jumps back easy she says easy hon sorry. Reach down between her legs can't get anywhere her thighs

GAS STATION

are large her jeans tight she reaches down unbuttons her pants sits up off the seat pulls them off I do the same each of us in our underpants I lift up her T-shirt hold it up move down to lick and suck her breasts she's rubbing the back of my head. I make a motion to go down on her she stops me says don't she's having her friend sit up straight confused can she have sex she says it'll be fine it's near the end she just has to remove her pad reaches down into my underwear rubs my cock and balls I begin to stiffen and she goes down gets me fully erect working it up and down with her mouth. Now she sits up removes her panties I take the rubber from my shirt pocket I won't need it she reaches down to remove her pad when she does it makes a squishing noise of planks going into the muck-puddle rolls down the window tosses it out lays back down on the bench with her legs spread. I climb onto her but can't find my way in she reaches down takes it in her hand guides me at first it doesn't want to go then suddenly I'm inside pumping for all I'm worth ready to cum within a minute so I slow myself down so she'll enjoy it too don't cum too early pump slowly enough suck on her breasts and swap long tongue kisses suddenly Tommy's voice a banging on the side of the truck how the hell you doing in there. Tommy get the fuck out of here you asshole Annie shouts I hear Joe yelling for him leave us alone what an asshole you ain't kidding Annie says now I'm beginning to soften my cock slips out she stops it with her hand pumps down low near my balls until I'm hard pumping again if I wore a watch know how long I'm going so I can cum can't hold back as I'm cumming see the image of the woman fucking the pig in George's magazine. I shift and moan into a long kiss with her all I want is to lie back try to keep my softening dick inside her keep pumping until she's satisfied she says it's okay she's all set I ask her if she came too she says never ask a woman that. We dress ourselves in steam window silent darkness odor of the muck pile and Countess's shits hot August night sweat and beer breath mixes with sex smells cum blood and cunt. I'm worried I did her all right you were pretty good she says really yes. She's first out I follow we walk the planks the muck swells up and over them *squishlup* each of our steps. My eyes are hypersensitive to the bright office lights I'm feeling tipsy from the beers a little sick to my stomach Joe fills all our beer cups Annie finishes up says gotta go walks over kisses me before she leaves the guys want to know how it went I tell them everything I can recall Joe says sounds like I did just fine. I thank them all Tommy says don't thank me thank George only reason Annie consented was they got George to agree to take her out again if she did me she just can't get enough of that huge thing swinging between his legs. Because it's my birthday I don't have to be home until eleven it's not yet nine I walk looking for my friends to tell them everything but they're not around the usual haunts home early parents out go upstairs fill the bathtub with warm water dried bloodstains on the bottom of my T-shirt can't put it in the hamper my mother will see it and ask questions roll it into a ball put in a paper bag I place in the bottom of the trash barrel outside. Back upstairs dried blood specks on my shriveled cock and on the inside of my left thigh I slide into the full warm tub submerged to my neck.

LET'S TAKE A ride I want to talk I'm in trouble must be something I've done at school sometimes Mr. D'Evani my math teacher comes in tells him I need to concentrate more I'm goofing off but he's nervous if he's pissed he'd show it I hop in the Jeep he drives to the pond road halfway around pulls over and shuts the engine. Tom Riordan's been talking about a state job for him might come up in the not so distant future I'll be a senior next year and then graduating if he sells the business he can make a little money for all his years of work there and have a chance to work a job where he can wear a clean shirt and have a retirement plan 'cause he's not getting any younger and there's no retirement plan with the station but he knows I might want the station and if I do want the station he won't sell and when I finish school I can come on with him though who knows what will happen since there's talk that the Jenney Oil Company's being taken over by the Cities Service Company otherwise known as Citgo. Don't know what to say he's never talked to me this serious before I have no idea he's thinking about all of this stuff I fantasize about running the station someday but when would it be my station and no longer his? Last Sunday at Jerry Hastings's house listen to new records Hendrix and Cream and Velvet Underground Jerry plugs in his electric guitar cranks up the volume in paisley bell-bottoms Nehru shirt shaking his long blond hair wails. I imagine being at the station the rest of my life all the long hot afternoon days of summer and cold wet snowy slush-down-my-back mornings of winter the pump tumblers clicking away endless gallons and dollars and cents out there something's stirring like bottom-of-the-barrel burning trash. I don't really want the gas station but I'm scared as hell where I'll end up though I might get drafted and have to go to Viet Nam Jerry says he's not going even if he's drafted he wants to start a band and without the station on my back I'll have more time to practice. What does my mother think I ask she thinks I should sell the station so we'll have some money to retire with otherwise who knows what will happen. He's fidgeting with his hands and fingers looking down at his lap and won't make eye contact with me hoping I'm certain that I don't want the station and I don't. Are you sure yes I'm sure. He stares out his window at the pond then looks down at his hands still fidgeting well then if you're sure you don't want it because if you do want it I won't sell.

HE'S LESS AND less interested in the station, business declines if Blackie can get some help from the bank he's going to buy my father out. Countess is gone all morning last time I saw her she was sleeping her usual spot back of the garage Blackie saw her drinking from her water bowl about ten. After lunch I walk up to the pond nose around surrounding woods' roads empty beer cans a used condom pair of women's underwear no sign of her back up Oak Street to the heights down Fulton Street cut back across Brackett past Jimmy the barber clippers and comb in hand standing at his barber chair man sitting in the chair several waiting anyone seen Countess no. Up to Cousin Lucy's apartment she's on the phone her full-volume shouts I had that damn trifecta in my apron and the son of a bitch tripped in the stretch. She hasn't seen Countess all day commands a good view of the neighborhood from her kitchen window late afternoon my father returns from the track he's worried calls the pound maybe she was picked up by the dogcatcher no. I make another sweep of the pond one of the lifeguards is securing the lifeboat says he saw her around sometime during the day but isn't sure when. I walk back down Oak to the Fellsway and Route 28 sound of cars and trucks whipping past on Interstate 93, alert neighborhood folks coming in for gas or walking past close the station at nine my father says that maybe someone stole her she is a full-blooded German shepherd on the way home we cruise the neighborhood once more. This morning bring the oil and window washer stuff to the pumps, take out the jacks, tire displays, windshield wiper display, air hose. Flick on the compressor *varoom* steady drumming MDC police cruiser pulls into the yard Johnny the MDC cop gets out Countess's choke collar in his hand says someone jogging around the pond this morning found her dead on one of the trails the officer isn't certain but it looks like she's been poisoned. Poisoned who would poison her oh there are a lot of sick folks out there Johnny says we can have an autopsy done to know for sure but my father will have to pay he says no. A van rolls in across the hose who would poison the dog thoughts of Countess dead and stiff through the night what pains she might have suffered swallow hard my choking throat eyes tearing fill up the van into the office run the charge card through my father sits back in his swivel chair shakes his disbelieving head at Blackie says I feel like I lost a son.